"You're determined to see me as a villain."

Adam shook his head sadly as he continued, "Has it ever occurred to you, Felicia, to wonder why?"

"What do you mean?" she said.

"You figure it out. Have I ever lifted a finger to harm you? What have I ever done to make you dislike me?"

"I don't dislike you," she assured him.

"But you won't go out with me. So," he asked with a lift of his shoulders, "what's the real reason? Isn't it possible the problem might be with you?"

"I don't have a problem!" she snapped.

But she was struck by how close he had come to the truth....

Rosemary Hammond lives on the West Coast but has traveled extensively with her husband throughout the United States, Mexico and Canada. She loves to write and has been fascinated by the mechanics of fiction ever since her college days. She reads extensively, enjoying everything from Victorian novels to mysteries, spy stories and, of course, romances.

Books by Rosemary Hammond

HARLEQUIN ROMANCE

2601—FULL CIRCLE
2655—TWO DOZEN RED ROSES
2674—THE SCENT OF HIBISCUS
2817—PLAIN JANE

HARLEQUIN PRESENTS

802—THE HABIT OF LOVING
859—MALIBU MUSIC
896—LOSER TAKE ALL
985—ALL MY TOMORROWS
1017—CASTLES IN THE AIR
1136—ONE STOLEN MOMENT

Model for Love

Rosemary Hammond

Harlequin Books

TORONTO • NEW YORK • LONDON
AMSTERDAM • PARIS • SYDNEY • HAMBURG
STOCKHOLM • ATHENS • TOKYO • MILAN

Original hardcover edition published in 1988
by Mills & Boon Limited

ISBN 0-373-02968-3

Harlequin Romance first edition March 1989

Printed in U.S.A.

CHAPTER ONE

FELICIA stood at the window of her loft apartment looking out through a grimy window at the busy city street below. She had the telephone propped in the crook of her neck so that she could use both hands to spray the jungle of plants that filled every available space in that corner of the room.

'I'm sorry, Carol,' she said into the telephone, 'I can't possibly make it to that reception on Saturday. I'm simply swamped getting ready for the exhibition on Sunday afternoon.'

'You have to go,' Carol said flatly at the other end of the line. 'And I happen to know quite well that you don't have another blessed thing to do at the gallery. Remember, I was the one who helped you pack up everything and deliver it. Besides, how would it look if the famous Felicia Fairleigh, prominent sculptress of ballet figurines, didn't care enough about the hand that feeds her to show up at a party in her honour?'

'Famous!' snorted Felicia, carefully wiping excess drops off a fatsia leaf. 'Prominent!'

'Well, you are,' Carol insisted.

'Hardly. At least, not yet.' Although her graceful clay dancers were beginning to win her a fairly secure niche in the art world, Felicia knew quite well she still had a long way to go for real success. 'Besides,' she went on, 'you know I hate ballet.'

'That's entirely beside the point,' Carol snapped.

'I don't have anything to wear.'

'Felicia . . .' Carol said in a warning tone.

'Oh, all right, I'll go to the party. But do I have to sit through two hours of dancing?' Felicia shuddered. 'And music?'

Carol laughed. 'It won't kill you. Sleep through it if you want. You just have to be there.' She sighed deeply. 'It beats me, though, how a person with your ability to create such beautiful works can dislike every other form of art so intensely.'

'Not *every* other form, just ballet. All those people hopping and twirling around makes me seasick. And as for the music, it's just a lot of noise to me.'

'That beautiful music!' Carol chided sadly.

'Can I help it if I'm tone-deaf?'

'Well, anyway,' Carol went on in an accusing tone, 'I would have thought you'd want to come, if only to watch me dance.'

'Carol, I've been watching you dance all my life. You know quite well you were the inspiration for my figurines in the first place. I've always loved the positions, the gestures, I just hate sitting . . .'

'You're my oldest friend, and you've never even been to one performance,' Carol broke in.

Felicia immediately sensed real hurt beneath the light, bantering tone. 'I'm sorry, Carol,' she said quickly, 'I'm being a selfish pig. I do want to see you perform, and I said I'll come. I'll even shout ''Bravo''—or is it ''Brava''?—at appropriate times.'

'Well, I'm only in the corps.'

'That's all right. You'll be the prima ballerina one day.'

'Fat chance of that, with Irina Petrovska dancing

rings round the rest of us!' There was a short, mournful silence. 'Well, anyway,' she said, brightening, 'I'm glad you're coming on Saturday. And who knows? You might even enjoy yourself.'

'Right,' Felicia replied drily. 'And my gardenia plant might bloom one of these days too.'

Carol laughed, prepared to be generous now that she had won her point. 'Well, it might. And in case you have any plans to conveniently "forget" about the party, I'll make sure to remind you tomorrow night.'

'I'm sure you will,' returned Felicia. 'Probably several times!'

They hung up then, and Felicia finished up her spraying. Although she did feel a little guilty that she had never once gone to see Carol dance professionally, she also knew quite well that she had been very cleverly manipulated into attending a party she had sworn she wouldn't—not to mention the performance—and she hated that trapped feeling.

She put away the empty sprayer in the cupboard underneath the window-seat, lifted Felix, her elderly male tabby cat, off the cushion, and and sat down to mull over her conversation with Carol.

The party was on Saturday. Today was Wednesday. That gave her three days to get used to the fact that she really did have to go, as promised. She knew she should be grateful for the honour. As her sculptures had begun to achieve a certain popularity, the City Ballet Company had benefited from her modest success in increased public support, both in ticket sales and endowments, and Saturday night's gathering in her honour was their way of showing their appreciation.

She'd have to go, and that was all there was to it. She had no real excuse not to. Every piece she intended to exhibit on Sunday had already been safely delivered to the Madison Avenue Gallery, and there was nothing more for her to do except show up.

Idly scratching Felix's ears, she surveyed her loft with satisfaction. It was everything she had hoped it would be, a little eccentric, perhaps, she thought, but meeting all her aesthetic and practical needs admirably.

The windows were double-glazed, shutting out the clamorous New York traffic noises from the street below, and Felix's loud purring filled the room. 'I know just how you feel, old boy,' she murmured aloud. 'We've got a pretty good life, you and I. But now,' she said sternly, setting him back down on the cushion and jumping to her feet, 'it's time to get to work.'

The studio end of the huge room was lit by a row of curtainless windows on the north side of the building, as well as a skylighted sloping roof. This work area could be separated by a line of heavy curtains that hung from floor to ceiling, giving her privacy at night as well as more homelike feeling.

During the day, however, the whole vast room was exposed at all the windows, north and south, for maximum light. This arrangement was also a constant reminder that there was work to be done, and gave Felicia the nudge she sometimes needed to get at it.

Since her work had started selling steadily, she was branching out in a new direction, and had begun to receive private commissions. She was tired of the ballet dancers anyway, and her present project was the head of a young boy, both a pleasure and a challenge.

Unwrapping the damp cloths from around the half-finished bust, she frowned critically at it. The hairline was not quite right, and she was simply unable to figure out why. As she studied it, however, comparing it to her preliminary sketches on the nearby easel, the original conception gradually worked its way down into her hands, and in a few moments, without conscious thought, her fingers began to remould the damp clay almost of their own volition.

For the next two days Felicia worked virtually non-stop on her young boy's head, stopping only to eat and sleep. She always kept her cupboards and freezer well stocked for just such a contingency, and had disconnected the telephone so that she wouldn't be interrupted. Now that she *knew* what had to be done, nothing must interfere with her work until the bust was finished, or, as sometimes happened, her inspiration ran dry again.

By late Saturday afternoon she was just putting the finishing touches on the clay mould when an insistent, annoying thought started to nag at the back of her mind. No matter how hard she tried to dismiss it, it kept coming back, and finally she was compelled to stop and pay attention to it.

She stood back and flexed the cramped muscles of her fingers. It was time for a break, anyway. Leaving the studio, she went into the kitchen alcove on the south side of the room to make a cup of coffee. It wasn't until she had poured the water in the pot and set it on the stove that it came to her.

The ballet—the reception afterwards! She had forgotten completely about them. She didn't even know what time it was. It was already just beginning to grow dark, but that didn't tell her anything, since it was early September and the days were growing shorter. She didn't own a clock or a wristwatch, so she plugged in the telephone and dialled the number for the time.

'At the tone, the time will be——' a pause, the sound of a soft beep, '—seven o'clock exactly.'

'Seven o'clock!' she cried aloud. Felix, stretched out on the rug in front of the window idly licking a paw, blinked at her. The ballet started at eight—she'd never make it. She had nothing to wear. Her hair was impossible.

Calm down, she told herself, take it one step at a time. A bath first, she decided, and dashed into the bathroom to run the water, tearing off her smock, her old grey sweatshirt, her torn stained blue jeans as she went.

While she bathed, she mentally went through her wardrobe, but it depressed her so much that she concentrated on her hair. That wasn't much better. She got out of the tub, dried off, and gazed at herself in the bathroom mirror. It was pretty hopeless, she decided, as she surveyed the untidy honey-blonde mop. Maybe if she washed it . . . No, there wasn't time. She'd just have to twist it up on top of her head, as usual, and let the shorter strands in the front that framed her face fall where they may.

'Clothes,' she said, and made a dash for the

wardrobe in her bedroom alcove. Several clean smocks, more blue jeans on hooks, some blouses and a few casual dresses. 'Surely I own a long skirt,' she muttered to Felix, who was sitting on her bed taking another of his endless, meticulous baths.

At last she found it, tucked way in the back, hardly ever worn—a black wool. It would just have to do. She torn it off its hanger. With a pretty white blouse and her good pearl ear-rings, the outfit would pass as formal wear.

Half an hour later she had locked the door behind her and run down the two flights to the street to hail a cab. It was still touch and go, but with luck she just might make it.

'Lincoln Center,' she directed the driver, 'and please hurry!'

When they arrived, Felicia thrust more than enough at the driver and ran across the pavement towards the entrance, past the fountain in the courtyard, past the outdoor restaurant, deserted now. In her haste, she almost tripped in the unaccustomed high heels.

Inside, the orchestra had already started the overture, and as she followed the silently disapproving usher into the darkened theatre down the aisle to her row, she realised with a sharp pang of dismay that she was going to have to disturb several people to get to the one vacant seat, which naturally was right in the centre.

Muttering *sotto voce,* 'Excuse me,' over and over, stepping on one woman's coat and tripping over the long legs of the man in the seat next to hers, she finally managed to sink into her own seat with a sigh of relief.

On the way over in the cab she had made herself a stern mental resolution to try very hard to enjoy the performance, but in just five minutes she knew it was hopeless. The ballet was a modern one, the music written by an iconoclastic young contemporary composer who never seemed to hit upon the few chords Felicia recognised, and who apparently was firmly committed to achieve as strident and clanging a dissonance as possible.

The dance itself was in modern dress, so that she didn't even have the lovely costumes of *Swan Lake* or *The Sleeping Beauty* to enjoy. There was an awful lot of hopping around and thumping up and down on the stage, and she couldn't for the life of her find Carol in the corps de ballet.

At the intermission, she stayed in her seat and dutifully studied the programme while everyone else stampeded out into the lobby for a drink. The second half would apparently include a solo performance by Irina Petrovska as a dying swan, or something. At any rate, when it started up again, Felicia noticed that there were an awful lot of white feathers in her costume.

She gathered that it was a brilliant performance from the rapt attention of the rest of the audience, but it was so long, so slow and drawn-out, that after ten minutes of it her eyes began to glaze over and a familiar creeping paralysis stole over her. Her mind began to wander and her eyes gradually closed.

The next thing she knew, she was being jolted awake by a burst of thunderous applause, and her eyes flew open. Her first conscious thought was,

Where am I? Her second, Thank God it's over. She still had the party to face, but with luck she could put in an appearance and slip away early.

The audience had risen to its feet by now, shouting, stamping their feet, and calling out to the graceful Irina, who was taking a curtain call. The first of many, Felicia thought ruefully, as she came out of her stupor and struggled to her feet.

As she did, her programme and her small beaded handbag both dropped on the floor at once. Before she could stoop down to retrieve them, the man who had sat next to her, the one whose long legs she had tripped over on the way in, had swiftly bent over, picked them both up and handed them to her.

'Thank you,' she murmured under her breath, and gave him an apologetic smile.

When she saw the stern, accusing look on his face, she thought, Oh, Lord, he's a ballet fanatic and is furious at me for going to sleep! Then she saw his lips quiver slightly.

'You were snoring,' he said in a low, amused tone.

'I was not!' Felicia countered hotly.

He raised one dark eyebrow and grinned openly at her. 'Oh, yes, you were.' Then he leaned closer, so that he could mutter in her ear, 'I don't blame you.' He turned from her then and started to make his way out into the aisle.

Felicia could only stare after him, open-mouthed. Then she had to smile. A kindred soul, she decided, heaving a grateful sigh, probably dragged to the ballet against his will by a culture-loving wife.

She kept an eye on him as he walked up the aisle towards the exit. He was a most attractive man, and so tall that she could easily spot his dark head above the crowd. A fine skull too, she mused, using her sculptor's eye, and with very interesting facial bones.

There was also something vaguely familiar to her about that head. She stared after him, searching her mind, but she couldn't quite put her finger on where she had seen it before. Then, when he finally disappeared from view along with the others into the lobby, she dismissed it and moved out into the aisle.

The vast theatre was emptying fast, and Felicia made her way up a wide, carpeted ramp to the Patrons' Lounge, a comfortable room just off the loge section on the second floor. There was a bar set up inside and several round tables lining the walls. It seemed to be full of people already, and as she stepped inside a burst of applause greeted her.

She smiled diffidently and had just turned around to see if someone important had come in behind her so she could get out of the way, when Sasha Malenkov, the director, came striding towards her.

'Felicia, my dear,' he said in the loud tone of voice that was normal for him. He put his arms around her and kissed her wetly on the mouth, then took her by the hand and led her firmly over to the bar, where he picked up a spoon and banged it loudly against a glass. 'Here she is,' he called to the crowd. 'Our own Felicia Fairleigh!'

It was then that she realised that the applause had been for her. She bobbed her head awkwardly and gave the crowd a nervous smile, hoping against hope that Sasha wasn't going to make a speech. But she should have known better. Sasha wouldn't miss an opportunity like this for anything.

She stood beside him, inwardly writhing with embarrassment, as he began extolling her artistry, her contribution to ballet in general and the present Company in particular; as he spoke, she wished fervently that she was anywhere in the world but here.

When it was over at last, there was more applause. Sasha kissed her again, and this time he kept his arm around her waist. Finally she spotted Carol in the crowd that was now clustered around her. Firmly removing Sasha's hand, Felicia managed to elude his grasp and moved towards her friend.

'See,' she said, clutching Carol's arm, 'I did come!'

'I'm proud of you.'

Felicia leaned towards her. 'Now can I go home?'

But Carol drew back and glared at her. 'You just got here! Come on, have one drink. You don't want to hurt their feelings.'

They walked over to the bar and ordered glasses of champagne. 'Well,' said Carol when they had been served, 'what did you think?'

Felicia took a long swallow of her wine. 'Um—I thought it was—er—interesting.'

Several people she knew began drifting towards her now, complimenting her on her work, congratulating her for her achievement in the service of the ballet, and with the familiar faces surrounding her she began to feel more at home, even to enjoy herself. To her relief, no one even mentioned the fact that this was her maiden appearance at the ballet.

Suddenly there was a slight commotion near the back entrance of the room, then a hushed silence, as all heads turned in that direction, and Felicia craned her neck to see Irina Petrovska making her grand entrance. She was a rather small woman, but her presence always dominated every room she entered. Smiling and nodding her dark, poised head at the worshipful crowd, she made her way straight towards Felicia, still standing at the bar.

'Darling Felicia,' she called, extending her hands gracefully before her, 'how lovely to see you at the ballet at last!'

Felicia cringed inwardly at this reference to her past failure to appear at any performance whatsoever, but put on a fixed smile and allowed the petite dancer to embrace her and brush her cheek lightly against hers.

It was then that she glanced at the man behind Irina, who was obviously her escort. As their eyes met briefly, Felicia recognised him instantly as the same man who had sat next to her in the theatre and accused her of snoring.

At the remembrance, her face immediately went up in flames, and she wished with all her strength that she could somehow sink through the floor or vanish miraculously out of sight.

Irina released her, turned to the man and put a possessive hand under his arm. 'Darling,' she said to him in her thick Russian accent, 'here is someone you must meet.' She gave Felicia a patronising look. 'Felicia, this is Adam St John, a great fan of the ballet.'

Felicia stuck out a hand and looked up at him. 'How do you do?' she said politely.

He was very tall, dressed in beautifully cut black evening clothes with an immaculate white shirt. His hair was thick and dark and perfectly styled to fall in a sleek, loose wave over that wonderful head. He was regarding her now with an amused half-smile on his lean face, and his eyes, an odd clear shade of greyish-blue with darker flecks in them, were fixed intently on her.

'How do you do?' he said with a slight bow.

For one fleeting moment Felicia felt a sharp pang of regret that she had been so careless of her appearance this evening. She had an almost uncontrollable urge to brush back the limp blonde bangs that were falling into her eyes by now and to straighten the untidy bun she had knotted so casually on top of her head.

In the next instant, however, she came to her senses. Although Adam St John was a devastating man, he was also of a type all too familiar to her. He held her hand just a little too long, the penetrating gaze was just a little too bold, and his practised charm just a little too obvious.

Every instinct warned her tht this man was a predator. An apparently successful one too, she added, judging from the way Irina was clinging so possessively to his arm. Familiar warning bells were clanging in her head, and she withrew her hand from his as though she had suddenly touched live coals.

His eyes widened imperceptibly, and then the smile broadened, as though he knew exactly what was passing through her mind. Ignoring Irina, who was graciously acknowledging accolades for her performance from a group of admirers, he took a step towards her.

'You *were* snoring,' he said in a low voice. Felicia opened her mouth to defend herself, but he was still speaking. 'Actually, I don't care much about ballet myself.' He paused, then added, 'Only ballet dancers. Are you a dancer, Felicia?'

'No,' she said curtly, a fact he had to know quite well after the display of boredom he had witnessed during the performance.

He eyed her critically. 'You could be.'

Just then Irina, her fans having dispersed at last, joined in the conversation. 'Felicia?' she cried with a little deprecatory laugh. 'A dancer? Heavens, no, Adam! Felicia makes all those pretty little statues of dancers. The party is in her honour, in fact.'

He frowned for a moment, then his eyes widened appreciatively as the light dawned. 'Of course,' he said, 'you must be Felicia Fairleigh.' She nodded briefly and he added, 'I admire your work very much.' His voice was deep and rather clipped, as though he was used to wasting very little time in idle conversation.

Felicia murmured her thanks, gave him a distant smile, and turned away from him to look for Carol. They had decided earlier to share a taxi home, and she was more than ready to leave. The long, boring ballet, coming on top of the intensive hours of work she had put in over the past few days, were catching up with her and she wanted nothing more than to go home, crawl into bed and sleep for a week.

She finally spotted Carol and had raised her arm to wave at her, when she realised that the man was still speaking to her.

'I'm sorry,' she said, turning back to him, 'I didn't

quite catch that. It's so noisy in here.'

'I said,' he repeated patiently, 'that I understand you're accepting private commissions now. In fact, I believe you're doing a child's head for a cousin of mine.'

'That's right,' she said. 'The Courtney boy.'

She gave him a closer look. If Adam St John was related to the wealthy Courtney family, he travelled in rather exalted social circles. But then, she thought, everything about him shouted money, from the top of his well-kept head to the tips of his polished black dress shoes.

'Come, Adam,' came Irina's imperious voice. 'It's time to leave. I'm very tired.'

'In a moment,' he said quietly. 'I'm speaking to Miss Fairleigh.'

'But I want to leave now,' Irina insisted.

Felicia had known the temperamental ballerina for several years now, ever since she had first started sculpting the dancing figurines that had been so successful. She was a Russian expatriate who had defected on a tour of America, and the darling of all the critics for the grace and beauty of her dancing. But her temper was legend, and Felicia could tell that she was sizzling now at Adam's unexpected refusal to do her bidding.

Although she couldn't help the little glow of pleasure it gave her to see Irina's orders challenged this way, she also remembered Carol's warning not to bite the hand that fed her. Irina Petrovska was a real power in the world of ballet, a world that provided Felicia not only with a growing reputation but a pleasant income as well.

'I must be going myself,' she said hastily. 'It was nice to have met you, Mr St John,' she added with a slight nod in his direction. 'Irina, thank you for the party.'

With that, she turned and walked away from them. There were certain to be fireworks, and she wanted no part of it. She finally did spot Carol standing near the bar talking to Sasha Malenkov and a group of other dancers, and Felicia made her way through the crowd in their direction.

'Sasha,' she said, when she had reached his side, 'thanks again ever so much for the lovely party. I'm dead beat, though, and it's time for me to go home.' She glanced at Carol. 'If you want to stay, I can go alone.'

Sasha had put an arm firmly around her waist and was leaning toward her, his face close to hers. She could smell the liquor on his breath and, from the way he pressed against her, she could tell that he'd had a little too much already. She sighed. Sasha tended to get amorous as he got drunk, and she simply couldn't deal with that tonight. She was too tired.

'One of these days, Felicia,' he was breathing at her, 'you will let me make a real woman of you.' His hands started to travel up and down her back, and he gave her another wet smack on the mouth.

Everything in Felicia was revolted. She stiffened and tried to pull away without offending him, laughing lightly to soften the sting of her abrupt withdrawal.

'Could be, Sasha,' she said. 'But not tonight, please.' She gave Carol a pleading glance. 'Well?

Are you coming or not?'

Carol set her glass down on the bar. 'I guess so,' she said, and stifled a yawn. 'It's about that time.'

After a long series of endless thanks and good-nights they were finally able to make their way out of the room, through the deserted house and outside to the wide courtyard in front. As they walked towards the street to hail a cab, Carol put a warning hand on Felicia's arm and held her back.

'What's up?' asked Felicia.

Carol nodded towards the kerb, and when Felicia followed her gaze she could see a man and a woman standing there beside a long, low limousine, apparently embroiled in a heated argument. When the woman's voice rose in anger Felicia recognised it instantly as Irina's, and she glanced at the tall man standing before her.

His arms were folded across his chest, and he merely stood there, motionless and mute, while Irina delivered her tirade. Then, without a word, he nodded shortly at her, turned on his heel, and strode off down the street, his hands in his pockets, his gait unhurried. Irina, virtually hopping, started to follow him, then stopped short as he hailed a passing taxi and got inside.

She looked after the taxi for a moment or two, then turned and got into the limousine, slamming the door behind her. As it pulled away from the kerb, Felicia and Carol glanced at each other, then both of them burst out laughing at once.

'I wonder what that was all about?' Felicia said at last as they continued on towards the street.

'I think perhaps Irina Petrovska might have met

her match at last,' Carol replied with a grin.

A taxi pulled up and they got inside. 'I doubt that,' Felicia said. 'I've never known Irina not to get what she wants.'

'Ah, but you don't know Adam St John.'

'No,' said Felicia, settling her head back wearily. 'Who is he, anyway? I know he's related to the Courtneys.'

'He's some kind of financial wizard, you know, one of those market analysts who trade in commodities or futures or something like that. Who cares? He's gorgeous, isn't he?'

'If you like the type,' Felicia said.

And you don't, I take it.'

Felicia gave a bitter laugh. 'It's very familiar, at any rate. I do know enough to stay away from it.'

'Oh,' said Carol, 'you're thinking of Kevin.'

'As little as possible,' Felicia returned drily. She shivered a little and closed her eyes.

After a short pause, Carol nudged her gently. 'I've been meaning to ask you something, Felicia,' she began in a hesitant tone.

Felicia yawned sleepily. 'Ask me what?'

'Were you serious when you encouraged Sasha tonight?'

Felicia's eyes flew open. 'Encouraged Sasha?' she exclaimed. 'When did I do that?'

'You know, when he said he was going to make a woman of you, and you said not tonight?'

Felicia was stunned. 'Of course I wasn't serious,' she said firmly. 'I was only trying to put him off without hurting his feelings.' Then the light dawned and she turned to Carol. 'Don't tell me *you're* interested in Sasha!'

'Well . . .' Carol hedged.

'I can't believe this, Carol. Sasha Malenkov? With his reputation? You're out of your mind!'

'That's easy for you to say,' Carol said hotly. 'Just because you're taken a vow of celibacy or something, it doesn't mean the rest of us are immune.'

Felicia still couldn't believe it. She supposed Sasha would be considered attractive to women. He was quite handsome in a rather frail, blond, Slavic fashion, and a brilliant choreographer, but he was famous for having bedded every possible attractive woman in sight, including most of the dancers in his company.

She shook her head. 'Well, Carol, it's your business. But you should know you can't take a man like Sasha seriously, any more than you can——' she searched her mind, 'any more than you can a man like Adam St John,' she finally came up with. 'They're like prowling beasts, just waiting to pounce on you and devour you.'

'Now, Felicia, just because you had one bad experience with a man, you can't lump them all together in a category like that!'

'Oh, yes, I can,' Felicia said with feeling. 'Believe me, I know the type. It sticks out all over them.'

They had reached her building, and by now she was sick of the whole conversation and anxious to drop it. 'Are you coming in?' she asked as she started to get out.

'I don't think so. I'm dead beat.'

'Well, goodnight, then. Will I see you tomorrow at the gallery?'

'Sure. And thanks for coming tonight.'

The loft was cold when Felicia stepped inside, but as she switched on the lights and surveyed the pleasant room, she felt a warm glow of satisfaction. Felix rose up from his position on the window-seat cushion, stretched widely, and with a great yawn jumped down to curl himself around her ankles.

'Good boy,' she murmured, reaching down to stroke his smooth coat. 'Are you hungry?'

He gave a loud purr in response, and she went into the kitchen to fill his dish. As he sat before it, delicately lapping up his dinner, she scratched the back of his head between his ears.

'We have everything we want right here, don't we, boy? Who needs a man to complicate things?'

Let Carol have Sasha and get her heart broken, she thought as she started towards her bedroom. Work was the important thing, and romance only a feeble illusion.

CHAPTER TWO

THE NEXT afternoon, as the first visitors began to trickle into the long, expensively simple gallery, Felicia had a sudden attack of nerves. What was she doing here? Her business was to stay at home and make statues, not stand around to be gawped at. She turned involuntarily to the tall, beautifully groomed woman at her side.

'Laura——' she began hesitantly.

The other woman smiled. 'A little stage fright?' she asked kindly, and put a hand lightly on Felicia's shoulder. 'Don't worry, it's to be expected, a perfectly normal reaction.'

'But do I really have to be here? I'm a sculptress, not a performer.'

Laura laughed and squeezed her shoulder. 'People like to meet artists,' she explained. 'You know that. Especially people with money to spend.' She waved a hand in the direction of the colourful display, laid out so carefully during the past week to show each delicate figurine off to its best advantage. 'It looks wonderful,' she went on. 'Quit worrying about it.' She dropped her hand. 'Now, I must go and greet the paying customers. Relax!'

Felicia watched Laura walk away from her towards the growing crowd as though her one source of security had suddenly given way. There was a sinking sensation in the pit of her stomach, and she reached out a hand to steady herself on the display table. She wished she had Laura's confidence, but then it wasn't *her* work so nakedly on exhibit.

'Relax,' she muttered to herself. Then, as a group of people began to drift slowly in her direction, she made herself smile.

She knew she was extremely lucky to have been asked by the manager of the prestigious Madison Avenue Gallery to exhibit a sample of her work. When Laura had called her a month ago with the invitation, she had been beside herself with joy. A few such shows and her reputation would be made. She could begin to concentrate seriously on the work she really wanted to do.

What she hadn't realised, however, was what an excruciating experience it would be to have to stand there and meet prospective buyers. Working in clay was a solitary occupation, and she was definitely not temperamentally suited for public performances.

The enormous room was filling up now, and growing quite noisy. Soft music played in the background, something classical Felicia couldn't begin to recognise with her tin ear, and at the far end, a bar had been set up with bottles of champagne on ice and a white-jacketed bartender efficiently pouring it out into the rows of stemmed glasses that sat on the counter.

Somehow the appearance of such a large crowd gave her a little more security. Hers was not the only work on display tonight, although the theme was the ballet. There were paintings hung on the walls, scenes from the world of the dance by various artists, and everyone milled about from one exhibit to the other.

Several people had come up to Felicia's table by now, and while they examined her figurines minutely with a critical eye and murmured among themselves, they did appear to be a friendly crowd.

A stout, white-haired woman in a gorgeous mink coat approached her now and held out a hand glittering with diamonds.

'Miss Fairleigh,' she pronounced. Felicia nodded, took in a gulp of air and smiled. 'I want you to know,' the woman went on in patrician, cultivated tones, 'that I admire your work extravagantly.'

'Well, thank you,' Felicia replied. 'Thank you very much.'

'I am a great aficionado of the ballet, you see, and it's obvious to me from the delicacy and precision of your figures that they were created with the same kind of love and dedication.'

Felicia didn't know how to reply to that, so she only smiled and nodded her agreement, hoping that the woman's enthusiasm would extend to an actual purchase. Since all the mundane business transactions would be made by Laura, she'd probably never know.

As the woman turned away, Felicia saw a grinning Carol making towards her through the crowd, a champagne glass in each hand, held aloft so as not to spill them.

'Here,' she said, handing a glass to her. 'You look as though you could use this.'

'Is it that obvious?' Felicia murmured, reaching gratefully for the champagne and taking a large swallow.

'Only to me, I imagine,' Carol replied. 'You have my deepest sympathy.' She shook her head sadly. 'I feel the same way every time I get out on that stage to dance, even in the relative obscurity of the corps.'

'I feel so—so—naked,' Felicia told her, shivering a little.

Carol nodded solemnly. 'I know. But listen, it's going quite well. I've been hanging around Laura just to sniff out the lie of the land, and have heard nothing but praise for you.'

Felicia shot her friend a look of gratitude. 'Let's just hope some of them end up buying!'

Suddenly there was a little flurry at the entrance to the gallery, and several heads turned in that direction to see what was causing the commotion. Felicia craned her neck, trying to see over the crowd, but could only catch a brief glimpse of a man's dark head, some inches above all the others.

'I wonder what that's all about,' she said.

'Who knows?' Carol replied with a shrug. 'Well, I guess I'll go circulate. Can I get you some more champagne?'

'Sure, if you come this way again. I could use it.'

From then on, Felicia was so busy meeting people and answering questions that her earlier attack of nerves was completely forgotten. A few of them even enquired intelligently about her work, and in at least two cases there was the definite hint of a possible future commission.

The time passed quickly, and eventually the crowd began to thin out. Felicia watched them go with a sudden feeling of letdown. She was deathly tired by now, her feet hurt from standing so long in one position, and her jaw ached from smiling. Thank God, she thought, it's over at last. She turned and walked over to the bar for one last glass of champagne.

Laura had been kept occupied all evening with business transactions, so that it wasn't until the last stragglers had left and the door locked firmly behind them that Felicia had a chance to speak to her again. The other artists were busy packing up their things, and she was alone at the bar when Laura joined her.

'Well, Felicia,' she said, giving her an amused smile, 'was it worth it?'

Felicia sighed. 'I don't know, Laura—you tell me. How did it go?'

The smile broadened. 'Quite well. You've made a real hit—several sales, in fact—and a lot of people are interested in your work.'

Felicia heaved a sigh of relief. 'That's wonderful, Laura. And I really appreciate all your help and support. To answer your question, then,' she went on with a grin, 'yes, it was worth it.'

'Well, at any rate,' the older woman said with a smile, 'I would say your future is pretty well assured after tonight. Not only that,' she continued on a more serious note, 'but the owner of the gallery was quite impressed with your success tonight, and seemed receptive when I suggested the possibility of a one-woman show in the future.'

Felicia could only stare. 'Why, that's marvellous, Laura! I can hardly believe it.'

'Did you meet him?' asked Laura. 'He was only here briefly, and there was such a crowd, you may have missed him.'

Felicia shook her head slowly. 'I don't know. I doubt it. I met so many people, but I think I would have known it if one of them had been the owner.'

'He likes to keep a low profile, and not many people know that he owns the gallery—among other things, I might add.'

Felicia made a face. 'A great patron of the arts, I suppose.' She sighed. 'I feel such a fraud when people call me an artist.'

Laura raised her eyebrows delicately. 'But you *are* an artist,' she said.

'Well, I don't *feel* like an artist. Sculpting isn't an art to me in the sense you mean, it's just something I happen to do well that also pays the rent.'

Laura laughed. 'Actually, he'd probably agree with you. I'm sorry you didn't meet.'

'Maybe some other time. I'd like to thank him personally.' She finished off the last swallow of her champagne. 'Guess I'll be on my way, then, Laura, and let you go home. You must be exhausted.'

'Oh, I'm used to it by now. The owner pretty much leaves all the details of running the gallery up to me.'

By now Felicia was almost overcome by curiosity. 'Who is this mystery man, anyway?' she asked. 'Or is it a deep, dark secret?'

Just then, from behind them, came the sound of a click in the lock of the front door. Both women whirled around at the same time to see a tall man step inside, his head averted as he shut and relocked the door.

'Here he is now,' said Laure with a smile. 'You can meet him for yourself.'

As the man turned and started walking towards

them in a slow, easy gait, one hand in his jacket pocket jingling keys, Felicia could only stare, open-mouthed.

It was Adam St John! *He* was the owner of the gallery, the mystery man, the power behind the throne that held the key to her future in his hands. It couldn't be, she thought.

She turned to Laura, a question in her eyes, hoping there was some mistake, but the tall woman was smiling broadly and moving forwards to greet him.

'Adam!' she called, her voice echoing in the vast, empty room. 'Did you forget something?'

For a moment he didn't say anything. His glance flicked over Felicia, raking her up and down in a lazy, arrogant gaze that just bordered on insolence. That comprehensive assessment, however brief, left her squirming inwardly. There wasn't the slightest doubt in her mind that in those few seconds, behind his half-closed eyes, she had stood there completely naked.

A fleeting smile crossed his lips. He *knows*, she thought furiously. He knows exactly what I'm thinking. Careful, she said to herself. This man had enormous power over her whole future, and she couldn't afford to antagonise him. A mask settled over her face, and she gave him a bland smile.

'Miss Fairleigh,' he said with a brief nod of his dark head. 'Nice to see you again.'

'Mr St John,' she murmured.

He turned to Laura, who was standing there, open-mouthed, goggling at them. 'Actually, Laura,' he went on smoothly, 'I came back in the hope of catching Miss Fairleigh before she left. I want to have a few words with her. You can go on home now if you like.'

'Why, yes, of course,' Laura said. 'I was just leaving. Goodnight, Felicia, and congratulations once again.'

Before Felicia could say a word, Laura began walking hurriedly away from them, her high heels tapping on the polished floor. When she reached the entrance she grabbed her coat off the nearby clothes-rack, and Felicia watched, stricken, as she disappeared through the door, closing it firmly behind her.

After she was gone, the gallery seemed very quiet, almost eerily so. Felicia twiddled her glass nervously between her fingers, waiting for Adam St John to speak. When he remained silent, she turned to give him a closer look.

He was standing there as though he owned the building—no, she amended, the entire city of New York—dressed impeccably in a dark business suit, white shirt and striped tie, and groomed to perfection.

'You wanted to speak to me?' she finally managed to ask.

A slow smile spread on the wide, thin mouth, and he raised one heavy eyebrow. 'Would you like another drink?'

There was something vaguely menacing about the tall figure. She couldn't quite put her finger on it, but the way he stood there, the expression on his handsome face, the lift of the dark eyebrow, all reminded her of something unpleasant, something that could disturb her nice, orderly life if she allowed it to.

'No, thank you,' she said politely. 'It's rather late, and I should . . .'

'Well, I think I'll have one,' he broke in, and reached for the bottle of champagne, still sitting on the bar in its silver ice bucket.

As Felicia watched the large, competent hands pour the wine into the fragile glass, then raise it to his mouth, her apprehension gradually began to dissipate, and her workman's fingers started to itch familiarly.

What she wouldn't give to model that head, she thought fervently, no matter what kind of man owned it. His features were near-ideal, yet with just enough minor imperfections to make them interesting. The straight nose was perhaps a shade too long, the jaw a little too square and bony, but the mouth! She'd never seen such a beautiful mouth. It was wide and straight, set in a firm line, but with a full, finely sculptured underlip that curved sensuously, softening the rather hard features.

As he drank, he kept his dark gaze firmly fixed on her over the rim of the glass, and when he had finished he set it down on the bar and smiled at her. Immediately Felicia's uneasiness returned, and she eyed him suspiciously.

'I'm curious,' he said at last. 'How is a woman who obviously detests ballet able to create such beautiful clay dancers?'

Felicia shrugged. 'That's not so strange. You can love the shape and form of ships at sea and still dislike sailing on them.'

'Well, why not ships, then? Why dancers?'

'Well, since my family are all ardent ballet fans and

my best friend is a dancer, I've been exposed to it all my life. What interests me most is the human form, and the graceful poses of dancers are perfect for my purposes. I just don't like performances. I think, though, it's mainly the music. I'm tone-deaf.'

'I suppose that makes sense,' he agreed. He poured himself another glass of champagne and, while he drank it slowly, his cool, assessing eyes never left her.

'It's getting late,' she said. 'What was it you wanted?'

Adam St John cocked his head slightly to one side. 'I'd like to offer you a commission. You do accept commissions—you said so last night.' The arrogant smile broadened, and a mocking gleam appeared in the clear, blue-grey eyes. 'Surely you didn't think I sought you out for personal reasons,' he said primly with a shake of his head. 'I hardly know you.'

Felicia's first impulse was to stalk out of the gallery and slam the door in his face, but she resisted it firmly. Not only was she too properly bred to do such a thing, but, if he was serious and really did want to commission a work, she'd be a fool to turn it down merely because the man was so insufferably conceited. What did she care if he enjoyed making fun of her? He was wealthy, and he had important connections. That meant influence, and her budding career could use all the help it could get.

'What did you have in mind?' she asked.

He shoved his long, lean body away from the bar. 'Come on,' he said. 'I'll take you home and we can talk about it.'

'Oh, there's no need for that,' she protested,

instantly on gaurd.

'This is New York, Felicia,' he said with a lift of one heavy eyebrow, 'and it's late at night. Surely you're aware of how dangerous it is for young women to be out on the streets alone? Besides,' he went on, taking her lightly by the elbow and leading her towards the door, 'I'd like to see where you work.'

Felicia thought of the mess in her loft and groaned inwardly. 'Really, Mr St John . . .'

'Adam,' he said, and kept on moving. At the door, he took out his key and looked down at her narrowly. 'I can help your career enormously, you know,' he said in a low voice. 'If you'll let me.'

What *that* meant, Felicia hardly dared contemplate. She was stuck with him now, however. If he got amorous, she'd just have to pin his elegant ears back and risk letting her career go down the drain. The one certainty in her mind was that hell would freeze over before Mr Adam Conceited St John would find his way into *her* bed!

They didn't speak at all during the short taxi ride to her building. Felicia sat way over on her side, absorbed in her plans to get rid of him at the earliest opportunity, while he leaned back comfortably and gazed silently out of the window.

When they arrived at her building, he paid the taxi driver and they walked up the two flights to her loft. Uncomfortably aware of his tall presence behind her, she opened the door, and he followed her inside without a word.

After she had locked the door behind him, she leaned back against it and watched him as he stood in the centre of the living area, his hands in his jacket pockets, his glance darting all around the enormous room, taking in every detail.

Once again, Felicia simply couldn't take her eyes off his head. Although she was distinctly wary of the man personally, as an artist, she was filled with admiration for the shape of his skull, the bony structure of his jaw, the deep-set eyes, the strong nose, and she knew she'd give anything to model it.

'This is nice,' Adam said at last. 'Just what I'd expect an artist's home to look like. Is one allowed to see your studio?'

'No,' she said curtly, glancing at the curtained-off area to her right. 'That's strictly off-limits.' Pushing herself away from the door, she walked slowly towards him. 'Why don't you tell me about the work you want done?'

'Yes,' he said. 'May I sit down?'

'All right,' she said grudgingly. His presence in her living quarters made her jumpy. She wasn't used to having men in the place at all, much less strange men with Adam St John's disturbing good looks and proprietorial air.

He sat down on a straight cane-bottomed chair, blessedly free, Felicia thought with relief, of Felix's long hairs, and leaned back comfortably. He took out a packet of cigarettes and offered it to her.

She shook her head. 'No, thank you.'

'Do you mind if I do?' he asked.

'Not at all,' she replied, and while he lit up with a thin gold lighter she found him an ashtray and set it on the table beside his chair. Then she sat down on the edge of the nearby sofa and turned to him. 'The commission,' she prompted.

'Ah, yes,' Adam agreed, blowing smoke into the air, 'the commission.' He leaned forwards, bracing his forearms on his knees. 'I'd like you to do a bronze cast of Irina. A bust, I think—she has such beautiful shoulders.'

Felicia felt a sharp pang of disappointment. She had hoped he would want her to do his own head. Then she recalled the heated scene she had witnessed in front of the theatre last night, and wondered if the proposed bust was to be a peace-offering.

'Irina would be a wonderful subject,' she agreed. 'But I'm a little dubious about the bronzing. I haven't had much experience with that kind of thing.'

'The Courtneys tell me you're doing their boy in bronze.'

'Yes, but I've yet to see how it will turn out.'

'I have the utmost confidence in your ability,' he said smoothly, stubbing out his cigarette. 'When can you start?'

'Don't you want to know how much I'm going to charge you first?' Felicia asked drily.

'All right. How much are you going to charge me?'

She named a figure that was at least double what she was charging the Courtneys, and watched him carefully to see if he would flinch at it. But the urbane expression on his face never wavered, and he nodded in agreement.

'That sounds fair enough.'

'I won't be able to start until I finish the Courtney job, and that won't be for another week at least. I should be done with the model by Friday, but I'm going out to Long Island for the weekend and won't be able to work on again until Monday.'

'You have friends in Long Island?'

'My family lives there, on the North Shore.'

'I have quite a wide acquaintance myself on Long Island, but I don't recall any Fairleighs,' said Adam.

'I'm not surprised,' she commented drily. 'I doubt if your acquaintance includes family doctors.'

His eyes widened. 'Of course,' he said. 'Dr Fairleigh is your father?'

'Do you know him?'

'Not personally, but I've heard him spoken of many times. Some old friends of mine are neighbours.' He rose to his feet and stood looking down at her. 'That's all settled, then? Can I tell Irina you'll be ready for her tomorrow week?'

'All right.' Felicia got up and walked to the door with him. 'I'll call her to set up a definite time.' Then, recalling the quarrel she had overheard last night after the ballet, she added wickedly, 'I take it this is by way of an olive branch for her.'

She gazed up at him with a cool smile, hoping to find at least a flicker of chagrin on his face, but all she saw was the same expression of bland insouciance.

'Oh, no,' he replied smoothly. 'It's more in the line of a farewell token.'

She put her hand on the door-handle. 'I see,' she said in a dry tone. 'You're off to greener pastures.'

She sensed an immediate tautening of his muscles and an odd stillness in the man standing next to her. 'You could say that,' he murmured softly, and before she realised what he was doing, the dark head had come down, his large hands had gripped her firmly by the shoulders, and she was being soundly kissed.

She twisted away from him and backed off a step, then stood there, breathing hard, her arms rigid at her sides, her face red.

'How dare you?' she breathed. 'What gives you the right——' she spluttered helplessly. 'Who do you think you are, to come barging in here with some cock-and-bull story about a commission and then attack me?'

Adam's eyes widened and he stared at her. 'Attack you? Hardly an attack, Felicia.' Then he smiled and said mildly, 'Aren't you over-reacting just a bit? It was only a kiss, just a friendly token of esteem. To seal our agreement.'

The amused look on his face only infuriated her further. 'There is no agreement,' she cried. 'I wouldn't work for you now for—for—a million dollars!'

'Oh, I'll bet you would!'

He was laughing at her now, and that realisation worked to sober her into an icy coldness. She narrowed her eyes at him and folded her arms across her chest. 'Get out,' she said calmly.

Adam reached down to take hold of the doorknob and pull the door open. 'Certainly,' he said, but before taking a step he turned to her and gave her a careful look. 'If I apologise nicely, will you have dinner with me tomorrow night?'

'Not for a hundred million-dollar commissions,' Felicia said flatly.

'I've offended you,' he said. 'I'm sorry.'

'I seriously doubt that,' she said in a severe tone. 'Unless it's because you didn't get what you came here for.'

He cocked his head to one side and gave her a long, appraising look. 'And what was that?'

'Look,' she said with a sigh, 'I know this will come as a great shock to you, but I really and truly am not interested in your games. I know your type quite well, and it doesn't appeal to me in the least.'

'And what type is that?' Adam asked in a conversational tone.

'The type that thinks it's God's gift to the whole female sex,' she replied promptly, then began ticking off on her fingers. 'The type that can never take no for an answer. The type that's so conceited, so arrogant, so selfish . . .'

'Hey, wait a minute!' he interrupted, raising a hand in the air. 'In another minute, you'll hurt my feelings!' He smiled down at her. 'Shall we try again? I humbly beg your pardon for "attacking" you like that, and would be honoured if you'd have dinner with me tomorrow evening.'

'No,' she said flatly. 'Goodnight, Mr St John.'

He stared at her for several moments, then said softly, 'You really mean it, don't you, Felicia?'

She almost had to smile at the totally genuine look of amazement on his face, but that would only encourage him, so instead she nodded and said solemnly, 'Yes, Mr St John, I really do mean it.'

His expression hardened. 'Well, I think I know your type, too, Felicia,' he said in a low voice. 'And of the two of us, I think you just might have the worse problem.'

With that, he went out into the hallway and started walking slowly towards the stairway. Felicia stood looking after him, her mouth open, watching his graceful, unhurried stride. He didn't once look back. In a moment he disappeared from view, and she could hear his footsteps going lightly down the stairs.

She was tempted to slam the door hard, just to drive her point home, but there wasn't a doubt in her mind that he'd surely recognise such a childish gesture for what it was. Instead, she closed it quietly, locked it securely, then started pacing the long room, literally gnashing her teeth.

'That man!' she muttered aloud. 'That insufferable man!' What right did he have to come barging in here with his fairy-tale about a commission, attack her like that, and then on top of it insult her with his innuendo about her 'type?

Yet, she thought, as her pace slowed, it wasn't really an attack. She rubbed the back of her hand over her mouth where he had kissed her, remembering the feel of his lips on hers, but as she did, anger flared again and she dropped her hand as though she'd been burned.

He *was* a most attractive man, she had to admit grudgingly. But that was just the trouble. Kevin had been almost as handsome, almost as devastating, and he had nearly destroyed her. When that little affair had collapsed she had made a solemn vow that she would never again be taken in by that kind of charm.

As she crossed over to the large south window to close the blinds, she caught a glimpse of her reflection in the darkened glass. What in the world he had seen in her to inflame his passion was anybody's guess.

She supposed she really should be flattered. Her

hair was pinned casually on top of her head, her one good dress was shapeless and out of fashion, and her fingernails were stained grey with the residue of clay that she could never quite get rid of, no matter how she scrubbed.

Obviously, Adam St John was the kind of man who felt it his duty to make a pass at every woman who happened to strike his fancy, and although Felicia was aware, from similar attempts in the past, that she seemed to possess a certain attraction for some men, she always guarded assiduously against any hint of careless body language, those little unconscious signals women send to indicate their availability.

She had dealt with the situation admirably, she decided at last, bruised the man's enormous masculine ego so successfully that she doubted very much he would trouble her again.

CHAPTER THREE

WHEN she woke up the next morning, Felicia had to grit her teeth and make herself roll out of bed at eight o'clock. Unused as she was to late hours, two nights in a row out until midnight left her still feeling she needed more sleep.

She had learned early on, however, that in solitary work a disciplined life was essential. Without some kind of pattern to her days, she would either become so involved in her work that she wouldn't even take time out to eat, or she would get no work done at all. Either way, she would end in chaos.

'A rule that's broken is no rule at all,' she muttered as she showered, dressed, fed a loudly complaining Felix and ate a light breakfast herself. She couldn't remember where she'd read that, but it had stuck with her, and she trotted it out often to spur her on when she would rather stay in bed.

Next on the agenda was tending the jungle at the window. Yesterday she had sprayed; today was the day to fertilise. As she stirred the proper solution at the kitchen sink and fed it into each voracious plant, Felicia congratulated herself on her fidelity to duty with a warm, self-righteous glow. With Felix and the plants fed, the bed made, the kitchen tidied, it was time to get to work.

She had just put on an old cotton smock and gone into her studio when the telephone rang. She always unplugged it before starting work, just so she wouldn't be tempted, but this morning she had forgotten.

She sighed, went back to the kitchen, and picked up the still-ringing telephone sitting on the counter.

'Hello,' she said brisquely.

'My, you sound grouchy this morning!' came her mother's voice. 'Did I catch you at a bad time?'

'Sorry, Mother. I was just on my way into the studio.'

'Well, that's al right, then,' her mother said complacently. 'At least I didn't interrupt your work. I called to congratulate you.'

'What for?'

'Why, your show at the Madison Avenue Gallery last night, for one thing, and the party in your honour on Saturday. It was in the morning paper.'

'Oh, really? It wasn't much. You know how dancers are. Sasha made a little speech about my "contribution to ballet," then they all spent the rest of the evening talking about themselves and their performance that evening.'

'How was it? The performance. I assume you attended.'

'I don't know. I went to sleep.'

'Oh, Felicia! How could you?'

Her mother was as ardent a ballet fan as Felicia was not, and was mystified by her daughter's strange antipathy towards it.

'No one noticed,' Felicia said. Then, remembering the tall man who had sat next to her, she added to herself—Well, not quite no one. 'Thanks for calling, Mother,' she said aloud. 'I'd better go get busy now.'

'You haven't forgotten you're coming out for your father's birthday next weekend?' her mother queried, adding, 'You did promise.'

'Of course,' she said. 'I'll be there on Saturday. Can someone pick me up at the train station?'

'I'll send Jack. He and Martha are coming down from Boston.'

Felicia sighed. Her brother and his wife were another pair of ballet maniacs, and she could just imagine how the weekend would go. There would be endless discussions of the latest productions, all of them probed in depth and with technical details that were a total mystery to her. At least, she thought, she'd have an ally in her father, from whom she had apparently inherited her tone-deafness and who was as bored as she was by ballet.

They hung up then and, firmly unplugging the telephone this time, Felicia went into her studio.

She worked steadily throughout the day, stopping only to give Felix his midday snack and eat a quick sandwich herself. The bust was coming along quite well, she thought, as she surveyed it critically in the fading afternoon light. She was still dubious about the complicated bronzing process her clients were insisting on, but at the same time she was eager to master a new technique.

It was an intensely exciting new venture for her, a departure from her usual style that was both challenging and a little frightening. Her work had improved dramatically since she had first started out just five years ago, fresh out of art school, improved to the point, she believed, where she could afford to gamble on the more expensive but more durable metal casting.

By Friday, the plaster mould was ready to be delivered to the metalworker, and as Felicia watched the man from the shop carry it out to his truck, she felt as though she were sending a beloved child out into the cruel world.

When the delivery truck was out of sight she turned from the window with a sigh of relief and regret. Pouring herself another cup of coffee, she sat down at the kitchen table to read the morning paper. She was looking forward to going home this weekend for her father's birthday. She needed a few days of total relaxation before she started on her next project, a commission from Bloomingdales for a series of ceramic ballerinas.

As she flipped hurriedly through the financial section on her way to the crossword puzzle, a photograph of a man caught her eye. Turning back a page, she stared down at an obviously candid shot of Adam St John. She glanced briefly over the article, which reported on a seminar he had recently conducted at Columbia University on the subject of dealing in the commodities market.

She returned to the picture again and gave it a more thorough look. It was a little grainy, but really quite good, she thought as she examined the casual pose. The man was as photogenic as he was good-looking. He was standing on the steps of a building at the university, speaking to a small group of students, one arm outstretched, a serious expression on his face.

It was the tilt of the fine head, however, that captured her attention. The strong chin was lifted up, showing the bony angle of his jaw, and his hair, ruffled in a slight breeze, softened his features. His stance was poised and graceful, his long legs slightly apart, and Felicia could well imagine the perfect, athletic body under the well-tailored clothes. It would really take a full-length statue to do him justice, something like a more mature version of Michelangelo's David.

Then she flushed deeply at the turn her thoughts were taking and firmly turned the page. Too bad that the external beauty of the man housed such a shallow soul underneath. As a man, he was definitely not her cup of tea, but as a subject for her sculpting expertise, he was near-perfect.

All during the rest of the day, as she caught up on her other work and got ready for the weekend in Long Island, that photograph of Adam St John kept returning to nag at her, until finally she simply had to go and look at it again.

She stood at the kitchen table staring down at it for a long time, her artist's mind buzzing insistently as she envisaged various ways of capturing the essence of the man's charisma in clay. Finally, hardly realising she was doing so, she tore the photograph out of the page and walked slowly into her studio.

Still in a trance, she pinned it to her easel. Then, without removing her eyes from it, she picked up one of her drawing pencils and began to sketch an outline of his head in sure, deft strokes.

An hour later she straightened up, exhausted, and stood gazing down at the drawing. It was really quite good, she thought with satisfaction, but perhaps it needed just a little more angle to the jaw. She picked up her pencil again, then stopped short, as it dawned on her what she had done.

Was she out of her mind? What demon had possessed her to do such a thing? She ripped the page from the board, crumpled it up and threw it into the wastebasket. Then she switched off her lamp and walked off without a backward glance.

Jack was at the Northport station to meet her, pacing up and down the platform, smoking. The train was fifteen minutes late, and as Felicia stepped off it, he strode forwards, glaring at her as though it was somehow all her fault.

'You're late,' he snapped, picking up her bag and moving swiftly towards the car.

'Well,' she said cheerfully, running a little to keep up with his long strides, 'and hello to you too, brother dear.'

Jack frowned down at her, then broke into a good-natured grin. 'OK—hello. How are you?' He opened the car door. 'Now get in.'

The house was less than a mile away, and in just a few minutes they were there. Jack, as usual, concentrated all his attention on his driving, which he did the same way he did everything else, in an absorbed, rather jerky manner. He sat hunched over the wheel, a fierce scowl on his face, muttering under his breath at the other Saturday morning drivers.

Felicia watched her brother with a faint smile of amusement. He was so predictable. She had been told they looked a lot alike, with the same slight build, the same darkish blond hair and hazel eyes, but there the resemblance stopped. Jack seemed to be in a state of perpetual motion, even when he was sitting still.

'How's the practice?' she asked as soon as he'd pulled the car into the driveway.

He turned to her and gave her a startled look, almost as though he was surprised to see her there. 'Oh, it's OK. The baby business seems to be booming in Boston.'

He was out of the car and walking up the front porch steps with her bag by the time she got out of the car, and she followed behind at her own slower pace.

Inside, the rest of the family were still gathered around the large oak table in the kitchen after a late breakfast. Felicia kissed her mother first, then turned to her father.

'Happy birthday, Dad,' she said warmly, and kissed him soundly on the cheek.

'Darling,' her mother said happily. 'You did come!'

'I told you I would,' Felicia replied.

'Well, Felicia,' her father chided, 'you have been known to forget at the last minute.'

'Forget your birthday?' she said, laughing. 'Never!' She turned to the dark-haired young woman sitting at her father's side. 'How are you, Martha?' she asked in a more subdued tone.

Even though she was actually very fond of her brother's lovely young wife, she often felt a little intimidated by her. The daughter of one of Boston's oldest socially prominent families, she had a patrician air of reserve that could be a little offputting at times. She was always beautifully groomed, with a perfect complexion and sleek black hair, the quintessential aristocrat.

She smiled now at Felicia. 'Quite well, thank you.'

Felicia turned to her mother. 'Am I in my old room?'

'Of course,' her mother said absently, and ran a hand

through her untidy grey hair. 'You don't mind sharing a bathroom with Jack and Martha?'

'Not at all. I'll just take my bag up . . .'

'I already did that,' said Jack, suddenly appearing at the doorway. 'Sit down and have a cup of coffee. Mother? I could use another cup myself.'

Felicia sat in her usual place at the family table where she could look out at the waters of Long Island Sound. It was a bright day, with a little chill in the air, and the Connecticut shoreline was clearly visible. Several sail boats dotted the water, their colourful spinnakers waving in the brisk breeze.

She loved the view of the Sound, just as she loved the rambling old house she had grown up in. Weathered grey by the frequent storms that battered that part of the coastline, and rather beaten up through the years by the four children who had been raised within its walls, every little nook and cranny, every shabby piece of furniture was familiar and dear to her.

As she sipped her coffee and gazed out at the view, she became dimly aware that her mother was speaking to her. 'Sorry, Mother,' she said, turning to her. 'What did you say?'

'I said,' her mother repeated patiently, 'that aside from celebrating your father's birthday, this was a wonderful weekend for you to come home.'

'Oh?' Felicia asked, helping herself to a cinnamon roll. 'Why is that?'

'The Bakers are giving a party tonight, and we're all invited. It's a benefit, very posh, to raise money for the ballet.'

'Oh, no!' groaned Felicia. 'Can't I even escape that here?'

Although far wealthier than her doctor father's family, the Bakers were old friends of many years' standing. They lived in a real mansion on the waterfront, and their parties were brilliant catered affairs that were attended by everyone in the upper strata of Long Island society lucky enough to receive an invitation.

'Felicia,' her mother scolded, 'that's no way to talk. The ballet has been very good to you.'

'So I've heard,' Felicia replied drily. 'From just about everybody I know.' She glanced at her father, whose mouth was twitching with amusement. 'Dad, are you going to let Mother drag you to this party on your birthday?'

He shrugged and raised his hands helplessly in the air. 'What can I do?' he asked. 'It's virtually a command performance. Of course,' he added with mock seriousness, 'if I get called out on an emergency, it won't be my fault.'

'Joseph!' his wife said in a warning tone.

'And if you need an assistant,' Felicia went on wickedly, 'I'll just have to go with you to help.'

'Oh, come on, you two,' Jack put in impatiently. 'It won't hurt you to go.'

'That's all right for you to say,' Felicia protested, turning on him. 'You actually *like* ballet—and dancers. I don't. Besides, I didn't bring anything to wear to a party. I'll just have to miss it, much to my sorrow.'

'Martha can loan you a dress,' her brother insisted. 'She always travels with a trunkful.'

Felicia had a mental vision of her sister-in-law's expensive wardrobe and gave her a stricken look. 'I couldn't possibly wear one of Martha's dresses!'

'Of course you can,' Martha said.

Felicia knew then that she was beaten, if even Martha would go so far as to share her clothes. It was time to be a good sport. 'All right,' she said with a sigh. 'Thanks, Martha, but I can probably find something in the wardrobe left over from college days.' She grinned at her father. 'Sorry, Dad. If you're called out on an emergency, it looks as though I won't be able to help you after all.'

Her mother looked so pleased by her decision that Felicia decided it was worth it. With that subject closed, Jack got up abruptly from his chair.

'I'm going for a sail. Martha? Felicia? Want to come?'

'Oh, yes, I'd love to,' said Felicia, rising to join him. 'I'll just run upstairs to change.'

Much to Felicia's mother's chagrin, and the amusement of the rest of the family, her father *was* called out on an emergency late that afternoon, and although he returned in plenty of time to attend the Bakers' party, it was after ten o'clock by the time they set out from home.

The Baker house was ablaze with lights when they drove down the winding road towards the beach, and music drifted out on to the evening air. The front was jammed with expensive cars, and Jack had to park some distance away from the imposing entrance.

The minute they stepped inside and were effusively greeted by their hostess, Mary Baker, Felicia was sorry she hadn't accepted Martha's offer of a dress to wear. Every woman there looked as though she had just stepped out of the pages of a fashion magazine.

Felicia had come up with an old red velveteen skirt from her college days and borrowed a white satin blouse, from her mother. In an effort to appear more festive, she had tied a red ribbon around the neckline of the blouse, but compared to the other women in their glorious plumage, she knew she stuck out like a dowdy sore thumb.

As she and her family made their way into the huge drawing-room, she saw immediately that most of the guests were all either dancers or ballet fans, naturally. Even the orchestra in the dining-room was playing tunes from the ballet—*Giselle,* her mother whispered to her, knowing Felicia didn't recognise one from the other.

Sasha Malenkov was in a corner of the room, speaking volubly to a group that included Irina Petrovska and Carol. The minute he saw Felicia, he came prancing towards her.

'How wonderful to see you, darling,' he called to her. He put one arm around her and managed to kiss her on the corner of her mouth before she could turn her head away. 'And your lovely mother. How are you, Mrs Fairleigh?'

Felicia's mother beamed. 'I'm fine, Sasha. You know my husband, of course. And this is my son Jack, and his wife. They're also great fans of the ballet.'

In order to escape Sasha's roving hands, while the introductions were being made Felicia drifted through the crowd towards Carol.

As she approached, she saw Carol's eyes widen in disbelief. 'Well,' she said drily, 'will wonders never cease! How in the world did you ever let them drag you here?'

'Oh, come on, Carol,' Felicia said uncomfortably. 'I'm not that bad, am I?'

Carol nodded vigorously. 'You're worse!' Then she smiled and linked her arm through Felicia's. 'But I'm very glad to see you, all the same.'

Felicia took a glass of champagne off a tray as a waiter walked past, and looked out over the crowd. Then, suddenly, in a far corner, she spotted the back of a familiar dark head. He was leaning over slightly, talking to a small group of people. Her first instinct was to turn away quickly so he wouldn't catch her staring at him, but she only stood there transfixed, unable to take her eyes from that perfectly shaped skull.

Then he turned around, almost as though he knew she was watching him, and their eyes met briefly. She hurriedly swallowed some champagne and turned back to Carol.

'What's he doing here?' she muttered.

'Who?'

'Adam St John.' Then Felicia recalled seeing Irina and remarked drily, 'I guess the hot romance is on again.'

'I don't think so,' Carol replied. 'At least, they didn't come together.' She gave Felicia an interested look. 'Why don't you like him? I think he's gorgeous.'

'And doesn't he know it!' Felicia breathed fervently. 'He took me home from the gallery last Saturday night, and talked his way inside with some cock-and-bull story about a commission. He couldn't even get out the door without making a pass. Which,' she added with satisfaction, 'I fended off nicely.'

Carol stared at her. 'Fended off! Are you out of your mind?' Her mouth curled in disgust. 'What is it with you, Felicia? What do you want from a man?

You're twenty-six years old, and except for that one ancient episode with Kevin, for all I know you've never even been kissed. Then an absolutely mouth-watering specimen like Adam St John comes along, and you . . .'

'Hold on, friend!' Felicia interrupted. 'In the first place, what makes you think I need a man in my life? And in the second, even if you're right, how can you possibly believe Adam St John would fit the bill? Can't you see what kind of man he is?'

'I sure can,' said Carol with feeling. 'He's beautiful and sexy and rich and . . .'

'And just like Kevin.' Felicia shook her head vigorously. 'No, thank you. Once is enough for me.'

'Well, I'm not going to argue with you,' Carol said, looking past her, 'but you'd better be prepared. He's headed this way.'

The back of Felicia's neck began to tingle, and she took a quick swallow of champagne. Surely, she thought, he wouldn't come anywhere near her after the way she had treated him? She looked at Carol, who, she saw to her disgust, was still smirking openly.

She just wouldn't acknowledge his presence, she decided irritably. What was he doing here, anyway? Tracking her down?

Then she heard his voice as he appeared at her side. 'Good evening, Felicia,' he said with a slight bow.

While Carol continued to goggle at him, Felicia pulled herself together and gave him a polite smile. She couldn't just ignore him.

'Hello,' she replied coolly. 'What a surprise to see

you here.'

Adam raised his eyebrows. 'The Bakers are old friends of mine,' he explained. Then he smiled. 'Surely you don't imagine I'm following you?'

Since that was just what she had been thinking, Felicia reddened a little and turned hastily to Carol to cover it up. 'I believe you've met my friend Carol Vincent.'

He nodded at Carol and gave her a pleasant smile. 'Of course—the dancer. I admired your performance last week very much.'

While Carol stumbled all over herself thanking Adam for the compliment, Felicia saw out of the corner of her eye that her brother and his wife were heading towards them out of the crowd, and heaved a deep sigh of resignation. She would have to introduce them to Adam.

When Jack and Martha arrived, she turned to them, but before she could open her mouth Martha had extended both her hands towards the tall, dark man with a cry of delight.

'Adam!' she exclaimed. 'How nice to see you here!'

Felicia watched, astounded, as her cool, reserved sister-in-law leaned over to press her cheek firmly against his. Then, still holding both his hands in hers, she turned to her husband.

'Jack, you remember Adam St John, don't you? He was at our wedding.'

Felicia searched her mind back to her brother's wedding, six years ago, but all she could remember was the enormous crowd that was jammed into the church in Boston, and the crush at the reception that followed it. She certainly didn't recall seeing or meeting Adam St John. At the same time, she also recalled that in those days she was so totally lost in her budding romance with Kevin Carruthers that she wouldn't even have noticed the existence of any other man.

Her parents appeared just then, and they too had to be introduced to the smiling Adam St John. As Felicia watched, her annoyance grew. She could see that her mother was falling firmly under his spell, and even Jack and her father seemed to be enjoying his company inordinately, laughing and joking with him as though they were old friends already.

Listening to their conversation, she gathered that Martha's older brother had gone to both prep school and college with Adam, and that their families were old friends. Wouldn't you know it? she thought irritably. Even in the bosom of her own family she wasn't safe from him.

She drew back a little to speak to Carol. 'Let's mingle a little,' she said under her breath, and moved farther away to chat with an elderly couple who were neighbours of her parents. The noise had grown much louder as the drink did its work, and in the next room people were beginning to dance to a small orchestra.

All this social whirl was beginning to get on Felicia's nerves. She longed to be back in her own quiet studio with only Felix and her plants for company, and when both the elderly couple and Carol left to join the dancers, she turned back to her family to see if by some miracle they were ready to go home.

What she saw, however, was that Adam was still

there, a bemused smile on his face. Beyond him, her whole family was staring at her, just as though waiting for a response of some kind.

'Well, dear,' her mother said, 'aren't you going to answer him?'

Jack grinned wickedly at her. 'Oh, you know Felicia. She's waiting to be coaxed.'

'I'm sorry,' she said at last, realising she must have missed something, 'I guess I was woolgathering.'

'I asked you if you would care to dance,' Adam said smoothly.

She didn't, of course, but when she saw the pleased look on her mother's face, and with Jack's nasty comment still ringing in her ears, she really didn't have much choice.

'All right,' she said stiffly, and allowed him to take her arm and lead her into the room where the orchestra was playing.

'So gracious,' he murmured in her ear as his arm came around her. 'I'm overwhelmed!'

'Listen,' she said, leaning her head back to look up at him, 'I didn't ask for this, you know. You had me trapped. You knew I wouldn't refuse to dance with you with my whole family standing there cheering you on.'

In reply, Adam only smiled at her and wrapped his arm more tightly around her. As he pulled her closer against his long, hard body, an undeniable slow warmth began to steal over her, and she drew back from him abruptly.

'Tell me,' she said, 'why are you really here?'

'I told you,' he said patiently. 'The Bakers are old friends of mine. I often attend their parties.'

'And you had no idea I would be here?'

His eyes widened. 'Don't you think you might be flattering yourself just a little?' he asked mildly.

'Then why did you ask me to dance?'

'It seemed like the polite thing to do,' he murmured, and began to execute a complicated step.

She immediately stumbled over his feet. 'Listen,' she said, planting herself firmly in place on the floor and refusing to budge, 'don't do that. Remember, I'm not a dancer.'

'Well, that's very obvious,' he said drily. He looked down at her feet. 'It *looks* as though there's one right one, but I could have sworn they were both left.'

Felicia drew herself up to her full height, and as she glared up at him she felt a sudden surge of longing to reach out and smack the complacent smile off his face. When he continued to grin down at her, she turned around with great dignity, ready to stalk off and *walk* home if she had to. But before she could move a step he had grasped her by the arm and turned her around bodily to face him.

'I'm sorry,' he said, barely able to contain his laughter, 'I couldn't resist. Truly, I'm sorry.'

She eyed him with suspicion. 'You don't act sorry.'

'Well, you'll have to admit, you haven't been very nice to me. I just needed to get a little of my own back. Male pride, you know.'

'Exactly what I was thinking,' she said sharply. 'And what law says that I have to be nice to you? I didn't invite you into my life. You're the one who barged your way into my studio, remember.'

'Could you raise your voice just a decibel higher?' Adam asked pleasantly. 'I don't think the people who live in the next block can quite hear you.'

Felicia glanced around uneasily. She *had* been speaking rather loudly. It was all his fault. She wasn't like this ordinarily. He brought out the worst in her, and she was just about to tell him so when she was suddenly arrested by the way he was looking at her, and the words died on her lips.

It wasn't so much the gleam in the clear grey-blue eyes or the half-smile on those chiselled lips, as it was the tilt of his head, the particular angle of his jaw. Once again her fingers virtually itched to capture that head in clay. No, she thought, bronze.

'What is it?' he asked at last. 'Is my tie crooked?'

'No,' she murmured. 'It's your head.'

Adam's eyes widened. 'My head?' He shook it a little. 'I'm afraid I can't do anything about that. I'm pretty well stuck with it as it is.'

She simply had to do it. There was no way out of it. If she didn't at least try, she'd regret it the rest of her life. Forgotten was the insufferable arrogance of the man, his conviction that all he had to do was crook a finger and women would fall panting at his feet. She felt driven by an irresistible compulsion.

'Would you sit for me?' she asked abruptly.

CHAPTER FOUR

FOR A moment Adam only stared blankly at her. Then his face fell. 'You mean, pose for you?' She nodded. 'That isn't exactly what I had in mind,' he murmured.

'I know what you had in mind,' said Felicia in a dry tone. 'Well? Will you or won't you?'

'That's my line,' he objected with a grin.

She could see then that she was wasting her time; he obviously had only one thing on his mind. 'Forget it,' she said, and turned once again to leave. 'It was a rotten idea.'

'Wait a minute,' he said, holding her back. 'Don't be in such a hurry. You're serious, aren't you?'

'I said to forget it. Now, let me go.'

'Don't be like that,' he said in a hurt tone. 'I rather like the idea of having my head immortalised. Let's at least find a quiet place where we can discuss it.'

Felicia eyed him carefully, thinking it over. 'All right,' she said. 'Let's go out on the terrace.'

They made their way through the crowd of dancers to the french doors that led outside. The evening was quite cool by now, and they had the terrace to themselves. Felicia walked ahead of Adam towards the low tone balustrade, and looked out over the wide sweep of lawn leading down to the Sound. The dance music drifted out, and from the shore came a whiff of salt spray, the low pounding of the surf.

The scent of late-blooming roses wafted up from

the garden below, filling the night air, and she drew in a deep breath. A thin crescent moon hung low in the northern sky, and the stars were blinking brightly.

She heard Adam come up behind her, but before she could turn around she felt his hands on her bare arms, pulling her close to him, and the touch of his lips on the back of her neck. Then, as his arms came around to encircle her midriff, his lips moved across her jaw, her cheek, to settle at the corner of her mouth.

In spite of herself, for just a moment, she allowed herself to lean back against him. The romantic setting, the music, the lovely late summer evening, all were working their magic on her, weakening her will to resist him. His warm mouth opened against hers, pulling at it, then closing over her lower lip, and when she felt his arm pressing against the underside of her breasts she knew it was time to call a halt.

She turned around in his arms and drew back a step from him. Immediately he reached out for her again, but she stood firm and gazed directly into her eyes.

'Adam,' she said sternly, 'before we can even begin to discuss this project, we've got to get one thing clearly understood.'

'Mmm?' he murmured, half closing his eyes and moving towards her to close the distance between them.

'No!' she said sharply, brushing his hand away. 'Will you please listen to me?'

He opened his eyes then and dropped his hands at his sides. 'All right,' he said with a sigh, 'I'm listening.'

'If you're going to sit for me, there is to be absolutely no emotional entanglement, no personal relationship between us.'

Once again he cocked his head at that devastating angle, and she drew in her breath sharply. The glow from inside the brightly lit room behind him cast a fascinating shadow on the plane of his jaw, and she held her breath as he leaned slowly towards her. He stopped when his face was only inches from hers, and gazed directly into her eyes for several long seconds.

Then he nodded briefly and straightened up. 'All right,' he said at last. 'If that's the way you want it.'

Before she could make up her mind whether she was gratified or disappointed at his agreement to her terms, there was a sudden commotion coming from the doorway, a crashing sound. Felicia looked past Adam to see Sasha, who was just righting himself after stumbling over a large terracotta urn near the house. Obviously quite tipsy by now, he was holding up a glass in one hand and waving at her with the other, and headed their way.

'Felicia darling!' he called as he approached. 'You haven't danced with me yet.'

He set his glass down carefully on the low brick wall beside him, then turned and put his arms around her, holding her close and blowing his pungent, warm breath in her face. Sasha was the last person she wanted to offend, and she stood rigid in his arms for a few moments, enduring the close embrace.

Finally, when his hands started roaming, she'd had enough. She pushed firmly at his chest. 'Sasha,' she said, laughing, 'you know I can't dance. I'll only trip all over your feet. I'm just on my way to the powder room, anyway.' Slipping out of his arms, she started moving away from him towards the house.

When she reached the doorway she suddenly heard Adam's voice calling to her. She'd been so preoccupied with disentangling herself from Sasha as gracefully as possible that she'd forgotten about him. She turned around to meet his amused gaze.

'You didn't say when you wanted me to come for my first sitting,' he said, walking up to her.

'Are you accepting my terms, then?' she asked, looking up at him with a stern expression. 'No involvement?'

'Sure,' he said easily, 'if that's the way you want it.' He paused for a moment, looking her over carefully. 'What is it, Felicia? Have you and Sasha got something going?'

'No,' she replied, flushing hotly, 'of course not!'

'What was that all about, then?' he asked with a toss of his head towards the terrace.

'If you know Sasha at all well, then you know that's just his way. It doesn't mean a thing.'

'Maybe not to you,' he said judiciously, 'but I wouldn't be so sure about Sasha.'

'Well, you'll just have to take my word for it. Nothing is going on, now or in the future. Not that it's any of your concern,' Felicia added tartly.

Adam thought this over for a moment, then nodded. 'If you say so,' he said. 'I just wouldn't like to think I was treading on another man's territory, that's all.'

'Adam,' she said in exasperation, 'I've already told you, there will *be* no treading. And you agreed, remember?'

'You're right, I did. But I do have one request of my own, however.'

'What's that?'

'That loft of yours seemed a little chilly to me. If I'm going to pose in the altogether, you're going to have to heat it up a little, or I'll come out all over in goosebumps.'

Felicia opened her mouth, then saw the glint in his eyes and snapped it shut. 'It's your *head* I'm interested in, not your body!'

His face fell. 'I'm crushed. Here I was, hoping . . .'

'Adam,' she broke in, 'on second thoughts, I'm not sure this is such a good idea.'

'I was only kidding,' he said innocently. 'You're so much fun to tease. Now, when shall we start?'

She thought a minute. The Courtney boy's head was safely at the bronzer's, and she wasn't really pushed for time on her next commission. She'd like to start right away, while the concept she had was still fresh in her mind.

'What's your scehdule like for the next month or so?' she asked finally. 'Could you give me a few afternoons a week?'

'I'm entirely at your disposal,' he said with a nod. 'Just say the word.'

'All right, then. How about getting started on Monday? Come early, around one o'clock, when the light is good.'

'It's a date,' he said.

On the way home in the car, it seemed the whole family was intent on nothing but singing the praises of Adam St John. Her mother, especially, was lyrical in her appreciation.

'Such beautiful manners!' she breathed. 'And such a handsome man!' She turned to her husband, who was driving. 'Why is it we've never met him before?' she asked. The slightly accusing tone of her voice made it seem as though somehow he were to blame.

'Don't know, dear,' he replied equably. 'You'll have to ask Martha. She's the one who knows him.'

'He's out of the country a lot, I think,' Martha explained from the back seat. 'At least, he was the last I heard. I really didn't know him that well. He was my brother Eliot's friend, not mine.'

'It seems to me you knew him well enough,' grumbled Jack.

Martha laughed at her husband. 'Why, Jack, you're jealous!' Still laughing, she said, 'There's really no need. I'm just Eliot's little sister to him. Besides, he had half the women in Boston in love with him when I knew him, and I doubt if that's changed, from the look of him.'

'Is he married?' Felicia's mother asked innocently.

'Not as far as I know,' said Martha. 'He seems to be a confirmed bachelor.'

'Well, I think he was a *very* nice young man.' Her mother gave Felicia a meaningful look.

'Not so young as all that,' Jack put in. 'Eliot's thirty-six, and if they were classmates, they must be the same age.'

'Well, that's young to me,' Mrs Fairleigh said cheerfully. 'Do you know where he lives, Martha?'

'Afraid not. Really, I know very little about him, except that he's supposed to have tripled the family fortune in commodities speculation, or something like that. I imagine he must have an office in Manhattan, but I have no idea where he lives.'

By the time they arrived back at the house, Felicia was

sick of the whole subject, and definitely regretting her rash decision to work with Adam. She should have followed her first instinct and run as far from him as she could get. Everything Martha had said about him only confirmed it.

Maybe it wasn't too late, she thought, as they straggled into the house. If he had an office in town, as Martha surmised, she could call him and cancel. Then she thought again about the lift of his head, the bones of his face, and she knew she wouldn't do it. Surely she could handle him if he got out of line, and after all, he *had* agreed to keep their relationship on a strictly business basis.

She said goodnight to her family and went upstairs to her old room. Later, as she lay in the dark, listening to the familiar, comforting bellow of the foghorn out on Long Island Sound, she considered the various poses she would like to try for their first sitting on Monday, then fell into a deep, dreamless sleep.

The next morning Felicia arose early and found her mother in the kitchen alone, sitting at the table and reading the Sunday paper. She looked up as Felicia entered the room and peered at her daughter over her bifocals.

'Would you like some breakfast, dear?' she asked, half rising out of her chair.

'Sit down, Mother. I'll just have some fruit juice and coffee.'

Her mother shook her head sadly. 'That's no breakfast. Why don't you let me fix you some eggs and bacon? Or pancakes—you always used to love my pancakes. I have some real maple syrup.'

'No, thanks.' Felicia downed a glass of orange juice, poured herself a cup of coffee, and sat down across from her mother. 'Where is everybody?' she asked, taking a section of the paper from the enormous pile.

'Oh, your father always sleeps in on Sunday. It's really the only day he has. Jack, too. You know these busy doctors.'

The two women read the paper and drank their coffee in silence for some time. It was another sunny day, and Felicia hoped Jack woud have time to go sailing again before he and Martha left for Boston. She herself planned to take a late afternoon train back into Manhattan, and hated to waste a minute of the clean fresh air.

Finally her mother closed the paper with a sigh and got up to refill her coffee-cup. She stood at the kitchen counter, her back to Felicia, who knew instinctively, from long experience, that the long sighs meant her mother had something on her mind. As she expected, she didn't have to wait long to hear what it was.

'You know, dear,' she said on her way back to the table, 'I was thinking this morning about that nice Adam St John.'

Felicia looked at her. 'Nice?' She had to laugh. 'Mother, that "nice" man is a predator on the prowl!'

'But he's so good-looking,' her mother insisted, sitting down. 'And so polite.'

'Oh, he's a charmer all right.' Felicia turned back to her section of the paper.

'You know, dear,' her mother persisted, 'you shouldn't judge all men by one bad experience. I realise Kevin hurt you terribly, but there are a lot of nice men in the world. I hate to see you settle for living alone the rest of your life.'

Felicia could only stare at her. 'Mother, don't you see? What I'm trying to tell you is that Adam St John is simply Kevin all over again—just as arrogant, just as selfish, and just as determined to have his own way at all costs, no matter who gets hurt. More so, in fact, and even more dangerous.'

Her mother was silent for several moments, then she sighed again. 'Well, dear, you might be right. It's just that he seemed very interested in you last night.'

'Oh, he's interested, all right,' Felicia said drily. 'In getting into my bed, to be perfectly blunt about it.' Her mother reddened deeply and took a quick swallow of coffee, and Felicia thought with satisfaction that that would probably be the last she'd hear about Adam St John for a while. 'Sorry, Mother,' she mumbled, 'but facts are facts.'

'Oh, that's all right.' Mrs Fairleigh put a hand on Felicia's arm and looked gravely at her. 'Do you ever hear from Kevin?' she asked quietly.

'No,' was the curt reply. 'Why should I?'

'Well, you were engaged, after all. I just thought . . .'

'The last I heard, he'd married the girl he jilted me for.'

'Oh, Felicia, that's a harsh word. He didn't really jilt you. In a way, he did the honourable thing, marrying the girl he'd made pregnant.'

'While he was engaged to me,' Felicia said bitterly. And sleeping with me too, she added to herself, even if it was only that one time, but she decided not to tell her mother that.

Jack came into the kitchen just then, yawning and stretching. He kissed his mother on the cheek and ruffled his hand through his sister's hair. 'If I can talk one of you two ladies into fixing me some breakfast, I'll take the boat out for a quick sail.'

Felicia gave him a dirty look and ran her fingers through her hair to straighten it out. 'Martha doesn't have you very well trained,' she said, rising from her chair. 'Haven't you learned to cook your own breakfast yet?'

'I'm a busy doctor,' Jack said complacently. 'I'm not supposed to cook for myself. Besides, you don't hear Martha complaining, do you?' He grabbed a handful of newspaper and buried his nose in it.

Felicia walked over to join her mother at the stove. 'I'll do it, Mother. Fair is fair.' She turned to her brother. 'I'll cook breakfast for you, but I'm going to hold you to that sail!'

All the way back into Manhattan on the train that afternoon, Felicia pondered the strange impulse that had prompted her to blurt out the proposal to Adam St John that he sit for her. Although her fingers itched to model his head, she wasn't so confident about his agreement to keep the rest of him to himself. By the time she got home, however, she was so certain he wouldn't show up anyway that her doubts were fairly laid to rest.

So when he appeared at her door on Monday afternoon, promptly at one o'clock, she was genuinely taken by surprise, not only because she really hadn't expected him to come, but because of the way he was dressed. Instead of the conservative, well-tailored suits she had seen him in before, he had on a pair of rather shabby jeans and a disreputable-looking sweatshirt.

He was also red-faced and perspiring, and she stared

at him in disbelief. He seemed far less intimidating and dangerous to her now. In fact, she thought, he looked quite boyish. His damp, dark hair fell loosely over his forehead and he was still panting.

'I've been running,' he explained without any preamble.

'I can see that.'

'I try to get in a couple of miles a day. Usually, I go back to the office to clean up, but I didn't want to be late for our appointment.'

'Well, now that you're here, you'd better come in.' Felicia opened the door wider, and he stepped inside.

'You look surprised to see me,' he observed when she had closed the door behind him.

'I am,' she replied.

'I told you I'd be here.'

'I know. I guess I didn't really believe you were serious about sitting for me.'

'I'm always serious about my commitments,' Adam said gravely. Then he grinned. 'That's why I'm so careful about making them!'

'I'm sure,' she said drily. 'Do you want to wash before we get started?'

'I don't suppose I could take a shower?'

Felicia wasn't so sure that was such a good idea, and she hesitated for a moment. On the one hand, she didn't want to give him any ideas about making free use of her apartment for his personal ablutions, but on the other, she really couldn't do much with him the way he looked now.

'Well, all right,' she agreed reluctantly. She led him to the bathroom and got out clean towels for him. 'But next time, start a little earlier so you can clean up at own place.'

'That's not nearly as much fun,' he said with a grin, and before she could think of a retort he had shut the door in her face.

Felicia went into the studio to get ready for the sitting, and as she sharpened her drawing pencils, she could hear Adam splashing in the shower—*her* shower—and singing a little off-key in a ringing baritone. The lead on her pencil broke, and she jammed it roughly into the sharpener, breaking it again.

By the time he was finished, the water turned off, the concert over, she knew she had made a terrible mistake to let this man into her apartment, into her life. For some reason, the image of him and what he was doing behind that door kept popping into her mind: the hard, well-muscled athletic body he was no doubt drying now, the long legs, the wide shoulders . . .

She finally managed to get a decent point on her pencil, but when she flipped over her drawing-tablet to a fresh page and tore an important sketch in half in the process, she decided she'd just have to tell him she couldn't do it. She was too busy, there were too many other demands on her time, she hadn't really meant it. She heard the bathroom door open and close, his footsteps coming towards her, and she turned around to face him, all primed to do battle.

But when she saw him, the words wouldn't come. All her objections evaporated and she could only stand there, the torn sheet still in her hand, and stare at him. Fresh from the shower, his dark hair still a little damp, the shabby jeans slung low on his lean hips, his broad, smooth chest bare, there was simply no way she could pass up the opportunity to capture all that masculine beauty in clay.

For a moment Adam stopped short and stared back at her, then came walking towards her. 'Sorry about the shirt,' he said. 'It was a little too grubby to put back on right away, so I'm airing it out at the window.' He grinned. 'Hope the neighbours won't get the wrong idea!'

'My neighbours are pretty tolerant,' Felicia replied. Then, pointing to a chair, she said, 'Sit down over there, please. I'll want to make a few sketches first from different angles. For now, why don't you fix your eyes on some point outside the window so I can get a three-quarter view. Just sit naturally and let your facial muscles relax. Don't pose.'

She started to draw rapidly, in quick, sure strokes, totally concentrated on the subject. The only sounds to be heard were the rasp of pencil on paper and the low, throaty purring of Felix, who was sunning himself at the window.

To Felicia's surprise, Adam was an ideal model. He sat perfectly still throughout the whole session, never asking a question, never complaining, and not fidgeting once. After half an hour of this Felicia set her pencil down, walked over to him, and stood gazing down at him through narrowed eyes, her chin cupped in her hand.

'I want to try it full face now,' she said under her breath.

He turned his head towards her. 'Like this?' he asked.

'No,' she said with a frown. 'Let me do it.'

When she put her hands on his bare shoulders to position them in the proper angle, his upper body immediately became totally pliable, allowing her to turn him in different directions, first one way, then another. His skin was warm and smooth to the touch, the muscles of his chest and shoulders taut and firm, and when she placed her fingers at the base of his long neck she could feel a little pulse quiver reflexively under her fingers.

'Sorry,' she murmured. 'Are my hands cold?'

'Not at all,' he said.

He glanced up then, and she found herself looking directly down into his greyish-blue eyes, the dark flecks sparkling in the sunlight. As he held her gaze in his, Felicia caught her breath, then stiffened, waiting for the clever innuendo, the sly suggestion, but he merely gave her a fleeting smile and turned away.

After that, whenever she had to vary the angle of his head or alter the slant of his shoulders, she could almost forget about him as a man and see him only as a subject.

And what a subject! she thought as she sketched him with sure deft strokes. By the time her fingers were too cramped to do any more, she had several different positions down on paper, all of them wonderful. Each one seemed to be better than the last, and as she stood back and surveyed the pencil sketches she had done, she knew she would have a hard time deciding which one to use.

'You can relax now,' she called to him, flexing her fingers and frowning down at her drawing-board.

Adam stood up and stretched his cramped shoulder muscles, then came walking towards her. 'May I see?' he asked.

'If you like,' she said, standing back to give him room.

He stood for several moments gazing down at the sketches, his face expressionless, masking whatever it was he felt. Then he turned to her and gave her a careful, thoughtful look. He didn't say anything for some time, and she began to grow uncomfortable under that clear, steady gaze.

'That's very interesting,' he said at last. 'Is that really how you see me?' He gestured towards the sketch pad.

'I don't understand what you mean,' she said, bewildered. 'I just draw what's in front of me.'

'Yes, but each person's particular vision of a subject is unique, wouldn't you say? For example, you wouldn't see a person quite as, say, Sasha would, or Irina, or your friend Carol.'

'You're probably right,' she said slowly. She gave him a puzzled look. 'I just don't quite grasp the significance of it.'

Adam raised an eyebrow. 'No?' She shook her head. 'Well,' he went on, 'it probably doesn't matter. Are we through for the day?'

'I suppose so. If that's all the time you can give me.'

'Do you want more?'

Felicia glanced out the window. 'It's still early. The light will be good for at least another hour.'

'Then I'll stay,' he said promptly. 'That is, if you intend to offer me some sustenance.'

She gazed at him in horror. 'You mean you haven't had lunch?'

'I never eat lunch. I had a late breakfast before my

run. What I had in mind was a cup of coffee.'

'Of course. It'll just take a minute. Why don't you walk around for a while? Get the kinks out.'

While she set on a pot of coffee in the kitchen alcove, Adam wandered around the loft, examining everything with concentrated interest. Then she heard him come up behind her and, when she turned around, she was glad to see that he had put his shirt back on.

'This is very nice,' he said appreciatively. 'I like the way you have it organised—efficient, yet comfortable. Lived in. You must spend a lot of time here.'

'Practically all of it,' she agreed.

'Doesn't that get rather boring?' He was standing close beside her now, and she moved a short step away from him.

'Not at all. I'm never bored.'

'Lucky you,' he said.

'Why? Are you?'

'Bored?' Adam thought a moment. 'No, not really. I'm like you, I guess, in some ways—fascinated by my work.' He gave a deprecating laugh. 'Although I'd hardly call it work!'

The coffee was finished by now, and as she poured it out into mugs she spoke to him over her shoulder. 'What is it exactly that you do, Adam? I've heard vague rumours that you're some kind of business tycoon.'

'Hardly that,' he said with a smile as he took the mug from her. 'I do deals.' She gave him a blank look. 'Which only means,' he explained, 'that I buy things—stocks, mainly, and commodities like gold or silver or wheat—when the market is low, and I sell them when it's high.'

'Ah,' she said. 'A good trick if you can do it. How do you know when these high and low periods are coming?'

'You don't—that's the fun of it. You guess.' He shrugged. 'It's an art too, I guess, in a way. At least, a good instinct for market fluctuations.'

'Sounds risky to me,' remarked Felicia.'

'Oh, it is—very.'

'And you don't mind that?'

He smiled widely. 'I thrive on it.'

'And what about the art gallery?'

'I speculate in art the same way I do the price of gold or a Broadway show. I enjoy making money. It's like a game to me, something I happen to be good at.'

She gave him a long look. 'That's funny,' she said at last. 'You just described my feelings about my own work. Everyone talks about my ''art'' as though there was some mysterious gift from the gods involved in it, or as though I had some lofty purpose in what I do.'

'And you don't have a lofty purpose?' asked Adam with a smile.

She shook her head vigorously. 'Not in the slightest. I went to art school instead of college because I had a knack for drawing and no ambitions whatsoever along the lines of academic achievement. Then, when I found out how much fun it was to work with clay and that people would actually *pay* me for it, the die was cast.'

He eyed her quizzically. 'Sounds to me as though you've taken a few risks yourself.'

'Why, yes,' she said slowly, 'I guess you could say

that.'

They finished their coffee then, and went back into the studio, where she worked for another hour, until the sun went behind the tall buildings of the city. Once again, Adam sat without moving a muscle the whole time.

'Right,' she said at last, 'I guess that's it for the day.' She glanced at him as he rose and stretched. 'You know, you're a wonderful model, as good as any professional I've had sit for me. It's a real blessing not to have to deal with sighs and twitches. The Courtney boy and I almost came to blows several times while I was working on his head!'

'I find it very relaxing,' he told her as he came to stand beside her to look down at the sketches she had done. 'So, what's the next step?' he asked.

'It all depends. I should probably do a few more sketches after I've had a chance to study these, then I'll build an armature roughly the size and shape of your head and shoulders.' He was standing very close to her now, and she gave him an uneasy sideways glance. 'Then I'll start slathering on the wet clay and hope to model a fair likeness of your features by the time I'm done.'

'Sounds like several weeks' worth of work,' he commented.

'Oh, at least. More likely several months.' Then she added quickly, 'But you won't have to sit for me that long. Once I get the sketch I want to use, I'll be pretty much on my own except for an occasional session just to make sure I'm on the right track.'

'I see.' Adam was silent for some time, gazing down at the drawing-board, as though trying to discover something there. 'Well,' he said, turning to her, 'how about some dinner? I'm starved!'

'Dinner?' she queried. What did he mean? Did he expect her to feed him? She was dead tired by now after the long afternoon's work.

'Sure. Why don't I go home and get changed, then I'll come back and we can go out somewhere. Do you like Chinese?'

'I don't know, Adam,' she said slowly. 'I'm pretty tired.'

'You have to eat,' he said in a reasonable tone. 'And you're certainly not going to work any more today.'

Felicia gave him a dubious look, but she had to admit she was tempted. The truth was, she thought with a sudden jolt of surprise, that she liked the man. He was good company, easy to be with, and wonderful to look at. What would be the harm? Besides, she'd made it clear that there was to be no personal involvement.

'You wouldn't even have to change your clothes,' he coaxed.

She looked down at her grimy, patched smock and well-worn blue jeans and burst out laughing. 'Right,' she said. 'Why don't we go somewhere really posh and expensive?'

Adam cupped his chin in one hand and eyed her judiciously. 'Well,' he said, 'you could wash your face, I guess.'

She raised a hand to her cheek, flushing with embarrassment as she suddenly recalled the streaks and smudges that always accumulated there while she worked. Then she raised her chin and smiled at him. Why should she care? She *was* a working woman, after all.

'Don't worry,' she said with a little laugh as she walked with him to the door, 'I might even comb my hair.'

'Oh, don't do that,' he said, looking down at her. 'I like it just the way it is.'

Their eyes met, and for a few seconds Felicia felt trapped in that clear, greyish gaze. A strange fluttering sensation arose in the vicinity of her heart, an unsettling feeling that momentarily threatened her equilibrium, and it was on the tip of her tongue to tell him she couldn't go out to dinner with him, after all.

But, before she could get the words out, he was on the other side of the door and walking down the hall. 'Be back in about an hour,' he called over his shoulder.

CHAPTER FIVE

IT WOULD be all right, Felicia told herself on her way into the bathroom to take her shower. The afternoon had passed quite pleasantly and without incident. She enjoyed working with Adam, liked him as a person, and there had been no sign of the arrogant predator she'd seen in him before.

Today he'd shown her a different side of his nature, a better side, one she felt comfortable with. There was no reason why they couldn't be friends. Surely, in this day and age, men and women could relate to each other on a platonic basis without all the messy business of romance to spoil things?

Then, just as she was about to step under the shower, her eye was caught by the towel he had used earlier, still hanging on the rack where he had left it, and still a little damp. All at once she could see him again in her mind as he had emerged from her bathroom, his chest and shoulders bare, his dark hair damp, every inch the quintessential male animal.

Averting her eyes hastily from the offending towel, Felicia stepped into the stall and was immediately pelted with a burst of icy-cold water. 'Damn!' she cried aloud, and had to catch herself from slipping on the wet tiles in her mad dash out into the bathroom.

Shivering and gasping, she reached back inside the stall and turned the cold tap down, the hot one on. When she finally got the right combination and stepped back under the warm spray, she gave herself a stern mental warning. If she had any hope at all of handling Adam, she'd better start by learning to control her own emotions.

An hour later to the minute, Adam appeared at her door, freshly shaven and wearing a well-cut pair of charcoal-grey trousers, a pale blue dress shirt open at the neck, and a pepper-and-salt tweed jacket. His Cordovan loafers were polished to perfection, and he stood before her looking as though he had just stepped out of the pages of a men's fashion magazine.

He gave her one swift, appraising glance and then nodded. 'Nice,' he said. 'You look very nice.' He reached out a hand and, without touching her skin, tucked a stray strand of hair behind her ear. 'That's better,' he said with a grin. 'Shall we go?'

For some reason, that small gesture sent a warm wave of satisfaction through her that she had taken some pains with her own appearance, in spite of the fact that her dark blonde hair never looked quite as neat as she would have liked. With hardly any expertise at all in using make-up, she had wielded a light hand—just a dash of cranberry-coloured lip-gloss and a light sprinkling of powder—and had worn a pale blue cotton shirtwaister dress that at least fitted her properly, was clean and pressed and had all the buttons sewed on. She brought along a darker blue cardigan sweater to throw over her shoulders in case it grew cooler later on.

He took her to a marvellous Chinese restaurant just a few blocks away from her apartment, well within walking distance, and as they strolled along the busy city streets Felicia noticed that, unlike some tall men—her own brother, for instance—Adam took some pains to slow his pace so that she could keep up with him.

While they gorged themselves on beef Mandarin and sweet and sour pork, they chatted easily together about their work, the pleasures and tribulations of living in the heart of Manhattan, their mutual dislike of ballet.

'I can take about five minutes of it,' Adam said halfway through dinner, 'and then dizziness sets in.'

'My sentiments exactly,' she agreed. She gave him a wicked glance. 'But you *do* like ballerinas.'

To her astonishment, he seemed a little put out by the tart comment. He frowned and waved a hand dismissively in the air. 'That was just talk. And believe me,' he added with feeling, 'definitely a closed chapter.'

An obvious reference to Irina, she thought, shovelling another helping of chow mein on to her plate. But she decided that the less said about the aspect of his life, the better, and continued to eat in silence.

'Besides,' Adam went on between bites, 'I only said that because at the time I thought you might be a dancer.'

She could feel his eyes on her, assessing her reaction to the provocative statement, but decided to ignore it. 'Since you went to school with Martha's brother,' she said to change the subject, 'I presume Boston is your home.'

He shook his head. 'Not any more. After my parents died I headed straight for the big city, and I've been here ever since.'

'Oh,' said Felicia sympathetically, 'you're an orphan then. No brothers or sisters?'

'Afraid not—a spoiled brat of an only child. My parents were very sedate, undemonstrative people, and quite elderly when they died. I was their midlife crisis,' he added with a grin, 'and I'd been out on my own for some time before they both passed away within a year of each other, so it really didn't come as a terrible trauma. Besides,' he said with another broad smile, 'they left me a nice chunk of old family money to play with.'

'It doesn't sound as though you were ever very close to them, then,' she commented.

'Hardly,' he said drily. 'All I remember from my childhood was rattling around that big barn of a place on Beacon Hill with only servants to play with. Other children were too noisy and too dirty, so until I went away to prep school I'd never really had a friend or been close to another human being.'

'That's sad,' she said, thinking of her own warm family life, the shabby house so full of young people while she and her three brothers were growing up, the smell of baking in the kitchen, the affection of her mother and father.

'Not at all,' he protested. 'Looking back, it was an ideal childhood. It taught me several very important lessons about life, real life, not the way it is in fairy-tales.'

Felicia looked up from her plate. 'Such as?'

'Such as the folly of thinking with your emotions instead of your head, of mistaking sentimentality for genuine conviction.' He paused. 'Shall I go on?'

'No, I don't think so,' she said slowly. She'd heard enough. The dazzling façade obviously hid a cold heart and a calculating mind, and she shivered a little at the thought of the things Adam had missed that he didn't even know existed.

He pushed his empty plate away, leaned back in his chair and lit a cigarette. 'Time out,' he said with a groan, then nodded at her empty plate. 'You certainly have a healthy appetite! Where in the world do you put it all? There isn't an ounce of fat on you.'

'Metabolism,' she said. 'The whole family's that way.' She polished off her last bite, then leaned back with a groan. 'I think I've had it, though. Full to the brim.'

'Tell me,' he said, eyeing her thoughtfully through a haze of cigarette smoke, 'what do you do with yourself when you're not working? I know you don't like music or ballet any more than I do, but surely you have some other interests outside sculpting?'

'Well, I enjoy sailing very much. In fact, I like all sports, but I don't get much chance to swim or play tennis in the city. My brothers and I used to ice-skate and ski when we were all living at home, but I haven't done much of either recently. I guess what I'd really like to do, if I ever have the time and money, is travel.'

'And where would you go?'

She laughed. 'You name it! I've never been anywhere. Born and raised on Long Island, I've been to New England on skiing trips and parts of Quebec—oh, and I spent one school vacation with an aunt in Philadelphia—but that's about it. A busy doctor doesn't have much time for taking his family sightseeing. How about you? Do you travel much in your work?'

'Constantly. You name it, I've been there.'

'And do you enjoy it?'

'Very much. I don't have a real home—never wanted one, to tell you the truth. I like travelling light, living out of suitcases, with nothing to tie me down.'

'It sounds to me,' she said softly, 'as though the only thing you don't like is permanence of any kind.'

'Yes,' he agreed promptly, 'you could say that.' He leaned back in his chair and gave her a thoughtful look. 'However, I don't like to think of myself as totally inflexible. It's possible I could be convinced to change that attitude.'

Felicia shifted uneasily in her chair and took a sip of water. Without looking at him, she said lightly, 'Well, I suppose miracles do happen.'

Adam reached across the table and put one finger on the back of her hand. 'Perhaps one day you'd come travelling with me, Felicia,' he said softly. 'I'd like to be the one to show you Rome, Paris, London, Athens . . .'

'Adam!' she broke in sharply in a warning tone.

He withdrew his hand with a sigh, then stubbed out his cigarette and glanced at the bill. 'Would you like a cup of coffee? A drink? Or are you ready to go?'

Suddenly Felicia longed to be back in the cosy warmth of her own apartment. Something about this man chilled her to the very marrow of her bones. He was an outsider, standing aloof and detached from everything that made life worth while, a drifter, a money-making machine. And the worst of it was, she thought, as she rose to her feet and followed him to the cashier, he hadn't the slightest conception of what he was missing.

The crowds had thinned out on the street by now. It was just past nine o'clock, too late for the dinner rush and too early for the after-theatre stampede. Although it was quite dark, with the hint of rain clouds in the evening air, the bright lights of the shops and street lamps that lined the pavement lit their way.

It had grown a little cool by now under the overcast sky, and when Felicia started to put on the sweater she had brought along, Adam reached over to help her. His large hands lingered slightly longer than necessary on her shoulders and, checking the impulse to pull away, she only thanked him with a brief, polite smile.

After that, they strolled along the few blocks in silence, and when they reached her apartment, Adam walked with her up the two flights to her loft without comment or asking permission.

At the door, she took out her key and turned to him. 'Thank you, Adam, for the dinner. I enjoyed it very much.'

The hallway was quite dim, with only one shaded bulb burning at the top of the stairs, a good twenty feet away from her door, and in the shadows she couldn't quite make out the expresssion on his face. She had the distinct feeling, however, that if she could see his face clearly she would find a familiar, slightly mocking smile of amusement on it.

'Aren't you going to invite me in?' he asked in a low voice.

'I don't think so,' she said, keeping her tone light and casual to mask the nervous tension that was building up in her. 'It's getting late, and I'm rather tired from the long afternoon. You must be too.' She put her key in the lock and looked at him. 'Can I have another sitting towards the end of the week?' She could hear the slight tremor in her voice, but was somehow compelled to keep talking. 'It will take me a few days to decide which sketch I want to use, and by that time I'll need . . .'

Out of the dimness she saw him raise his hand, then felt his fingers come to rest gently on her mouth, with no more pressure than the wings of a moth. 'Shh!' he said. 'Don't talk.'

As she stared up at him, mesmerised by the low voice, the dark hallway behind him, the silence, his fingers began to travel over her face, moving along to outline her lips, her chin. She felt the palm of his hand, soft and warm, cradling her cheek, then moving to grasp the nape of her neck, and trailing upwards to twine his fingers through her hair, propelling her head forwards at the same time.

She couldn't move, was scarcely breathing, her eyes held in that hypnotic gaze as his face came closer and closer, until finally his mouth came down on hers in a gentle back-and-forth movement that sent a sharp stab of pleasure through her whole body.

Mindlessly, she closed her eyes and allowed herself to slump against him. Both hands were on her face now, the thumbs moving up and down beside her mouth. His lips parted to tug gently at hers, then opened wider and closed again to deepen the kiss, while his fingers slid down to grasp her throat.

He was pressing her up against the wall now, his legs spread slightly apart and one arm around her waist, holding her to him. Felicia couldn't seem to make her mind function. All she was aware of was a blissful sensation, a sort of tingling warmth, spreading through her.

Then, at the same time, she felt the tip of his tongue glide past her lips and the hand at her throat slide slowly down to cover her breast. She froze instantly and jerked her head back.

'What's wrong?' he murmured.

Even in the gloom of the hallway she could see the glow in his half-closed eyes as he gazed down at her. His hand tightened on her breast, kneading gently, and his head came down again.

Before his mouth could connect with hers again, however, she twisted her head sideways and brushed the exploring hand away. Adam raised astonished eyebrows at her and reached out for her again, but she was too fast for him. Sidestepping quickly, she put her hand on the door and turned the knob.

'Felicia?' he said blankly. 'What's wrong?'

Tugging at her dress where he had disarranged it, and smoothing out her skirt, she drew a deep gulp of air into her lungs to steady her breathing and gave him a cool, direct look.

'You know, Adam,' she said, 'if we're going to work together, this just won't do.'

'Why not?' was the prompt reply.

'Just take my word for it,' she said drily.

He stared at her for several moments, a puzzled look on his face, then said, 'Is it me in particular, or men in general?'

'That's a loaded question, and I'm not going to answer it. Now, are you going to keep your hands to yourself from now on or not?'

He cocked his head on one side, as though thinking it over, then gave her a broad smile. 'No, I don't think so.'

Felicia pushed the door open and started to walk inside. 'Well then, there's no point in discussing it any further. We'll have to call the whole thing off. I simply can't work with someone who's *grabbing* me all the time.'

'Grabbing?' he asked incredulously. 'You call that grabbing? You enjoyed it—you know you did.'

She couldn't lie. 'All right, say I did. I also enjoy eating food ocasionally that isn't good for me or taking chances on a ski-slope. That doesn't mean I should keep doing it.'

'But you've already set a date. You can't back out now. I've had to rearrange my schedule to fit these sittings in.'

'Sorry,' said Felicia cheerfully. 'That's your problem.'

She started to close the door, but Adam put his foot firmly in the way, and she glared at him, anger building in her like a white-hot flame. She opened her mouth to protest, but he held a hand up, silencing her.

'All right,' he said. 'I'll be here as planned, with all my perfectly normal instincts held firmly in check.' He gave her a puzzled look. 'I don't see you at all as an easy mark, if that's what's bothering you. I don't operate that way. I like you—I admire you. I'm very attracted to you. What's so wrong with that?' He shook his head. 'I don't understand you, Felicia.'

'You don't have to,' she snapped. 'And I'm still not sure I want to go on with this project.'

Adam frowned down at her. 'Well, if it comes to that, neither am I. I'll come on Thursday at the same time, and we can decide then. In the meantime, if you feel you can't handle it, let me know so that I can make other plans.'

With a brief nod he turned and sauntered off down the hall. If he was anywhere near as angry as she was, she thought as she watched him go, you'd certainly never know it by the casual way he walked or the careless lift of his head and shoulders.

She closed the door quietly behind her and leaned back against it for a moment, thinking hard. With all the women at his disposal, why was he picking on her? He was so much like Kevin, they could have been twins. What was it with these gorgeous men that they had to seduce *every* woman they met?

Across the room she saw Felix sleeping on the crushed velvet armchair, the best one she owned and the only one that was forbidden to him. 'Felix!' she scolded, and clapped her hands sharply. He opened one eye and stared at her for a few seconds, then slowly uncurled himself and stood up. After a yawn and a stretch, he sat back down and proceeded to take one of his endless baths.

'Men!' muttered Felicia, crossing the room and picking him up bodily. Immediately he broke into loud purring, butting his head up under her neck. 'Men,' she said again, and carried him into the kitchen to give him his bedtime snack.

During the next few days, Felicia caught herself at odd moments—and far too often—pondering the question of whether Adam would show up on Thursday. She wasn't so sure she even wanted him to, and at least half a dozen times she made up her mind quite firmly that she didn't, until finally, on Wednesday afternoon, she marched to the telephone to call him and tell him so.

Then it dawned on her that she had no idea how to contact him. Clever Adam, she thought, telling her to call him if she didn't want him to come, then conveniently neglecting to give her his number. She started to dial Laura's number at the gallery to ask her for it, then changed her mind and set the receiver back down. Laura was so mesmerised by the man herself that she would guard his privacy as tenaciously as a lioness her favourite cub.

It would serve him right, she grumbled to herself on Thursday morning while she ate breakfast, if she just wasn't home when he came. *If* he came, she amended. Although he hadn't shown any overt signs of anger on Monday night, a flaming ego like his couldn't help but be bruised by her rejection. She could go to a film or do some shopping, or go to visit Carol.

She stopped short, her coffee-cup half-way to her mouth. Why should I leave? she thought angrily. It's *my* apartment. She set the cup down hard, got up from the table and started pacing around the vast loft until she found herself in the studio area, gazing down at the sketches she had made of him on Monday.

The trouble was, she brooded, she wanted to do the sculpture more than she'd ever wanted to do anything before. Already she had a good idea which pose she would use for the clay model, but she needed him here for the proper perspective, that essential dimension of depth, and the only way she could get it was by having the actual flesh-and-blood man here before her.

By twelve-thirty she was certain he wouldn't come at all. She couldn't really blame him. Although it had given her a great deal of satisfaction, that rejection must have been a bitter pill for a man like Adam St John to swallow.

But he did show up. Felicia had just finished a light lunch, picked up a clean smock and gone into the studio to get to work again on her commission for the dancer figurines, when she heard a knock at the door. With a slight but unmistakable quickening of her heartbeat, she ran quickly to answer it.

Adam stood there, looking wonderful in a well-pressed pair of tan chinos and a white shirt unbuttoned at the throat. Today he was not out of breath or perspiring, and she wondered if he had forgone his usual run. She opened her mouth to ask him, then decided against it. No personal conversation at all, she reminded herself, or it would never work. At least today there would be no fooling around about taking a shower. That too had been a mistake.

'Come in,' she said.

'You didn't call,' he remarked casually as he stepped inside, 'so I figured you wanted to go on with the project.'

'You didn't leave me your telephone number,' she said drily, crossing her arms in front of her and turning to face him.

'Oh, didn't I?' Adam seemed genuinely surprised. 'Sorry.' He reached in the pocket of his dark windbreaker, drew out a card and handed it to her. 'Here—you can always leave a message if I'm not available. I'm gone from the office a lot, but I have a wonderful secretary who takes excellent care of me.'

Felicia took the card from him, glanced at it, and set it down on a nearby table. Apparently he was leaving it entirely up to her. She could tell him to leave right now, and the whole affair would be over and done with, or ask him to stay. While she debated, he took a step back towards the door.

'I wasn't sure whether you expected me,' he explained. 'If you're not ready for me, I'll leave.'

I'll never be ready for you, she said to herself. He'd put the burden of decision firmly on her shoulders. Since either way it would constitute a victory of sorts for him, she might as well do what she wanted to do, what she knew she would do, all along.

'Well, I wasn't sure you'd come, either,' she said briskly. 'But now that you're here, shall we get to work?'

She led him into the studio and motioned for him to sit down in the usual chair while she put the clean smock on over her jeans and shirt. When she went over to turn his head and move his broad shoulders into the right position, he gave her one quick upward glance, but didn't say a word.

Once again he sat perfectly still throughout the whole first half-hour session, and Felicia worked with quick, sure strokes until she had roughed out the sketch she would finally use.

'You can relax for a minute if you want,' she said, her eyes fixed on the drawing-board.

Adam didn't say anything, but she could hear the scratch of a match as he lit a cigarette, and smell the smoke as it drifted her way. She frowned down at the sketch. Something still wasn't quite right. Perhaps just a little more lift to the chin. She stood back a pace, then gave him a quick look.

He was leaning back in the chair, his long legs stretched out and crossed in front of him, his arms folded over his chest, and gazing at her fixedly.

'Would you like to go to a charity ball at the Four Seasons with me tonight?' he asked the moment their eyes met.

'What's the charity?' she asked idly, still trying to decide on how to change the pose. 'A home for discarded mistresses of business tycoons?'

'That was unkind,' he chided gently. 'But you're not far off. It's a benefit for the Screen Actors' Retirement Fund.'

Felicia opened her mouth and stared at him. 'Are you serious?'

'About wanting to take you or the name of the charity?' he asked in a dry tone.

'What interest can you possibly have in retired screen actors?' she asked, ignoring the question. 'I thought your tastes ran more to methods of making money, not giving it away.'

'Let's just say I use my charitable contributions as a tax break, if it'll make you happy,' said Adam in a flat voice. He sat his mouth in a firm line, leaned over and ground out his cigarette in the ashtray at his feet.

'I'm sorry,' Felicia said tartly, 'but you'll have to admit you haven't exactly gone out of your way to impress me with your humanitarian impulses.'

He shook his head sadly. 'You're bound and determined to make me out some kind of heartless villain, aren't you, Felicia? Has it ever occurred to you to wonder why?'

'What do you mean?'

'You figure it out. Have I ever lifted a finger to harm you—or anyone you know of, for that matter? What have I really done to make you dislike me?'

'I don't dislike you,' she assured him.

'But you won't go out with me.'

'No, I won't do that.'

'Well then?' he asked with a lift of his shoulders. 'What's the real reason? Isn't it possible the problem might be with you?'

'Now listen, Adam,' she said heatedly. 'I don't *have* a problem, and I'm under no obligation to give you an explanation for anything I choose or don't choose to do.' She ran a hand over her untidy hair in exasperation. 'Besides, I've explained it all before. I can't do my work and carry on any kind of personal involvement with you at the same time. It just can't be done. Why won't you take my word for it?'

He nodded judiciously, not in the least abashed by her angry tirade. 'You're saying I might have come on a little too strong.'

'A little!' she exclaimed, raising her eyes heavenward. Then she gave him a stern look. 'Now, shall we get back to work?'

An hour later she had finally finished the sketch to her satisfaction, and it was time for a real break. She knew Adam must be numb from holding his position for so long, and she was tired herself. When they resumed later, she'd correct the proportions of the wire armature so that she could start working in clay.

'I think that's probably enough for now,' she said, laying down her pencil.

He stood up and started flexing his shoulder muscles backwards and forwards. As she watched him out of the corner of her eye, she thought once again how much she would like to do a full-

length statue of him, preferably nude, and in the next instant she could feel her cheeks begin to burn.

During her studies at art school, it had been common practice to work with nude models, both male and female, and there was never any embarrassment or hesitation about it in the almost clinical atmosphere of the studio. Somehow, though, she didn't quite believe it would be entirely wise at this point to ask Adam to take his clothes off, although she had no doubt that he would probably be delighted to do so.

'If you'd like to take a short break,' she said, 'perhaps you wouldn't mind giving me another hour later on this afternoon.'

'Sorry,' he said, 'I'm afraid I can't today.' He picked up his jacket from the back of his chair and put it on. 'I wasn't sure whether you'd want me to stay, so I made another appointment.'

He smiled thinly—the first time, Felicia thought, she'd seen him smile that afternoon—and started walking towards the door.

'Of course,' she murmured, following behind him, 'I understand. It can wait until next time.'

He turned around and raised an eyebrow at her. 'Will there be a next time?'

'Well, that's up to you. You know how anxious I am to do the statue, but if you don't feel you have the time . . .'

'I can make the time. But only with the understanding that I pay you for the head when it's finished.'

'You mean you want to buy it from me?'

He nodded. 'That's right.'

Felicia was taken completely by surprise. Her intention had been simply to use him as a model and perhaps exhibit the sculpture if it turned out well, so that if anything, she should be paying him. If he bought it from her, then it would no longer belong to her, and she wasn't sure she wanted that.

'I don't know,' she said slowly. 'I had planned to use it for my new exhibition.'

Adam shrugged. 'Can't you make more than one casting?'

'Yes, I suppose so. It's a slightly different technique, but I don't see why not.'

'All right, then, that's settled. When do you want me to come for my next sitting?'

'When are you free?' she asked.

'Any time you say. I keep a tight schedule, but I can make time for it.'

'How about Monday, then? Same time.'

'I'll be here,' he said, and crossed over to the door.

He had just put his hand out to open it when there came the sound of a familiar, rhythmic knocking and Carol's voice calling from the other side.

'Felicia? Are you in there?'

Adam gave her an enquiring look. She nodded, and when he opened the door Felicia could barely suppress a giggle at the wide-eyed look of astonishment on Carol's face as she looked up at the tall, dark man standing in the doorway. She stood there with one foot inside and her mouth hanging open, her eyes darting from Adam to Felicia, then back to Adam again.

With a nod of his head, Adam smiled down at her. 'Hello,' he said pleasantly. 'It's Carol, isn't it? The dancer.'

Carol immediately broke into a flustered, foolish grin that was the closest thing to a simper Felicia had ever seen, and batted her eyes up at him. 'Why, yes,' she cooed coyly, 'I remember you.' How could she forget? was the clear implication. 'You're Adam, aren't you? Adam St John.' She stepped all the way inside and glanced at Felicia. 'Am I interrupting something important?' she asked archly.

'Not at all,' was Felicia's cool reply. 'Adam is just leaving.'

Actually, although Carol's sudden appearance put an end to a rather awkward moment, she wasn't at all pleased that her friend had discovered Adam in her apartment. Somehow it seemed important to her to keep the project to herself.

She turned to him. 'Goodbye then, Adam.'

He flashed her one brief, knowing grin, then sobered instantly when he saw the look on her face. 'Goodbye, Felicia,' he said. 'I'll see you Monday.' With another nod at Carol, he went out of the door and closed it firmly behind him.

When he was gone, Carol just stood there for several moments, staring at Felicia. Then at last she put her hands on her hips and smirked openly. 'Well!' she said. 'What was that all about?'

'Nothing you'd find interesting,' Felicia replied airily. 'I'm only doing a sculpture of his head.'

'I don't blame you,' said Carol with feeling. 'It's certainly one of the best I've ever seen.' She eyed Felicia narrowly. 'Come on, friend—give! That's not all you're doing. I saw that look in his eye when he said goodbye to you.'

'Don't be ridiculous, Carol.' Felicia was beginning to grow very irritated with the whole situation. 'What are you doing here, anyway? I thought you were rehearsing every afternoon.'

Carol sighed. 'Sasha had to go to the dentist. He's been complaining about this awful toothache for weeks and putting off doing anything about it until finally we all ganged up on him and made him go. Some men are such babies,' she added.

'You mean *all* men, don't you?' Felicia agreed fervently. 'Well, now that you're here, how about a cup of coffee?'

When they went into the kitchen, Carol sat down at the table, braced her elbows on the top, cupped her chin in her hands, and stared fixedly at Felicia while she made the coffee. 'Now,' she said, 'tell me about Adam St John.'

'Carol, I already did. He's sitting for a bust, and that's all there is to it.'

'I don't believe you,' Carol said with a snort. 'Do you really mean to stand there and tell me you have this gorgeous man here in your apartment, all to yourself, with no competition in sight, and all you're doing is making a model of his head?'

Felicia nodded and sat down at the table. 'That's exactly what I mean.'

Carol leaned back in her chair and gazed with astonishment at her. Then she shook her head slowly from side to side. 'You know, that's a little weird, Felicia, even for a man-hater like you.'

Felicia bridled at that. 'I am *not* a man-hater!' she

protested hotly.'Some of my best friends are men. I don't hate my father or my brothers. I don't hate Sasha.'

'That's a cop-out,' Carol retorted promptly. 'You know quite well what I mean.'

Felicia gave her a stern look. 'If you mean that I've learned to be very wary of a certain kind of man, then I'll have to agree with you.'

'And Adam St John is that kind of man?' Carol asked.

'I think he's the mould the rest of them were made from,' was the dry retort. 'Thank God I've been inoculated against their charms, and I have only pity for the poor women who are foolish enough to fall in love with them.'

'I take it you're including Sasha in that category?' Carol said stiffly.

Felicia gave her a startled look. Carol was absolutely right, of course, but it wasn't exactly tactful of her to say so. 'Not necessarily,' she hedged. She got up to pour the coffee.

'Well,' Carol went on, 'I think you only developed that attitude as a defence against getting hurt again. Just because you had a bad experience with Kevin . . .'

Felicia whirled around with fire in her eyes. 'Now, back off, Carol,' she said in a warning tone. 'Kevin has nothing to do with this. That's ancient history.'

Undaunted, Carol forged ahead. 'Oh, really? Are you telling me, then, that there's no resemblance between Adam St John and Kevin Carruthers? Face it, Felicia, you have a fatal attraction for that kind of man.' She took a swallow of coffee and sighed deeply. 'I think most women do.'

'Not me!' Felicia exclaimed heatedly. 'Not any more. I'll never in a million years forget . . .' She broke off as a painful vision of the night Kevin had stammered out his sorry tale came into her mind. 'I should have known better than to fall in love with such a handsome man in the first place,' she finished up lamely.

Weak, too, where women were concerned, she added to herself, and unable to resist flattery. He and Adam were cut out of the same cloth. Both possessed the same mesmerising quality that blinded women to the shallowness underneath.

She knew she wasn't being quite fair to Adam by comparing him to Kevin, but she had been so badly hurt by that experience, had given her love and trust so totally, only to have it turn to dust and ashes in the end, that she was still almost paranoid on the subject.

As though she could read her friend's thoughts, Carol asked softly, 'Do you ever hear from Kevin?'

'Oh, heavens, no!' Felicia replied with a dry laugh. 'I hear *about* him occasionally from mutual friends in Hartford. Apparently he's still practising law, and the last I heard he and his wife have two more children.'

Carol shook her head sadly. 'What a rat! Imagine getting another girl pregnant while he was engaged to you. I still can't believe it.'

'Well, at least he married the girl. I suppose you've got to give him credit for doing the honourable thing in the end. It was probably best in the long run that it happened when it did. Sooner or later someone would have come along, and it would have been a lot harder to face after we were married.' Felicia gave herself a little shake. 'But that's ancient history.' She got up to get the coffee-pot and held it up. 'Have another cup?' she asked.

'No, I guess not. I told Sasha I'd pick him up at the dentist's, and he should be almost through by now. I'd better go.'

After Carol had left, Felicia went back into the kitchen to pour herself another cup of coffee. It was just beginning to get dark, and she stood at the window, sipping the hot coffee and looking out at the gathering dusk. One by one, the street lights started to come on. It was autumn already, she realised with a little shock of surprise. Almost October. Soon the cold weather would start, then the ice and snow, the short days.

Shivering a little, she wandered into the studio, turning on the lights as she went. She stood at her drawing-board, gazing down at her final sketch of Adam's head. It was perfect, she thought, just the right angle. She would do it in a slightly three-quarter pose, the head uptilted just a little, the long column of his neck and throat bare.

She set her cup down on her work table and went to the airtight plastic bin where she kept her clay. She took the lid off and unwrapped a fresh package, testing it for dampness, then carried it back to the table. Slowly, carefully, she began to lay strips of the clammy grey material over the metal armature she had adjusted that afternoon to the proper size and shape.

As she worked, far into the night, she marvelled again and again at how the cold, dead clay in her hands would eventually become an almost living, breathing replica of the man who was its model.

CHAPTER SIX

BY THE middle of October the work on Adam's head had progressed to the point where Felicia didn't need him to sit for her on a regular basis any more, and one Thursday afternoon, just as they were stopping for the day and she was wrapping the clay model in damp cloths, she made up her mind to tell him so.

'This can be our last session for a while,' she said, as he was putting on his jacket.

He had come in a dark business suit today, with a matching waistcoat, fresh, crisp, white shirt and subdued striped tie. With one arm inside his jacket, he paused and gave her a sharp look, then slowly slid his other arm into its sleeve. He straightened his tie and came walking slowly towards her.

'I see,' he said thoughtfully. 'Does that mean you're almost through?'

'Oh, no. It just means I can forge ahead on my own now. I will ask you for a few more sittings, but not for a while.'

'But, essentially,' Adam persisted, 'the—er—collaborative effort is at an end.'

'You could say that,' she agreed. She turned from him and patted the damp cloths more firmly around the clay model.

'Well, thank God!' he said with feeling.

Stung, Felicia whirled around to face him. Although she knew that the gruelling sessions must have been hard on him, still she felt a little hurt that he seemed so relieved to have it over with.

During the three weeks he had appeared on schedule every Monday and Thursday, sitting perfectly still throughout each session and hardly speaking to her at all, even in the short breaks. When they were through for the day, he would smile at her, perhaps utter a few pleasantries about the weather, and then leave.

'Has it really been that bad?' she asked.

'Oh, no, not at all.' He was walking towards her now, and smiling broadly. 'Only you promised to go out to dinner with me when it was over.'

Felicia stared up at him, open-mouthed. 'I promised no such thing!' she protested.

'Of course you did. Don't you remember? At the very first sitting, you laid down a rigid rule. No personal involvement so long as we were working together.'

'Well, yes,' she spluttered, 'but I didn't mean that would change when we were through.'

Adam gave her a hurt look. 'Well, you certainly implied it.'

She was about to assure him smartly that any inferences he drew from what she said were his problem, when it occurred to her that perhaps she was being a little unreasonable. How could it possibly hurt to go out to dinner with him?

She could feel his eyes on her, waiting for her answer. Could Carol be right? Was she being unfair to him—and to herself—by lumping him in Kevin's category just because there were similarities in the two men?

Besides, she did owe him something, and now that she knew him better, he didn't seem nearly as shallow as she'd first imagined him to be. No man could sit uncomplaining for hours at a time the way he had, nor honour her request to keep his distance, without possessing a pretty firm character.

There was no question of trusting him. Of course she couldn't trust him. He'd make another pass at her the minute she let her guard down. But she could trust herself, couldn't she? She just wouldn't let him get one inch past her defences.

'All right,' she said at last, 'I'll have dinner with you tonight.'

'Good,' said Adam with satisfaction. 'I have a little business to attend to this afternoon. Why don't I come back and pick you up around seven o'clock?'

'I'll be ready,' she said, and started walking with him out of the studio.

At the door he turned to her. 'And Felicia,' he said softly, 'wear something pretty and festive. We should celebrate the end of our business together and the beginning——' he paused and smiled down at her, 'of something else,' he added, and left.

They took a cab to a quietly elegant French restaurant in Greenwich Village, where the food was rich and perfectly prepared, the wine carefully chosen, and the service impeccable.

As he'd requested, Felicia had worn her most festive outfit, a very simple black silk dress, set off by a single strand of pearls and matching teardrop earrings that her parents had given her for her last birthday. Judging by the gratified look on Adam's face when he came to pick her up, apparently her appearance satisfied his expectations as well.

He was an ideal escort—courteous, attentive, and amusing. As he helped her on with her coat, his touch was firm and deft, but never lingered longer than necessary on her shoulders, and when they walked along the pavement in front of her apartment to hail a taxi, he held her arm lightly, even protectively, but with no hint of possessiveness.

At the restaurant, while they waited in the foyer to be seated and then followed the maître d'hotel to their table, Felicia couldn't help noticing the frankly appreciative eyes of more than one woman ogling his tall figure and fine dark head, but he seemed to be oblivious of their inviting glances and kept his attention fixed firmly on her.

After ordering drinks, Adam lit a cigarette, leaned his elbows on the table, and gazed appreciatively across the table at her. 'You look quite beautiful tonight, Felicia. That dress suits you—simple but elegant.'

She gave him a wry smile. 'Beautiful? Hardly that.'

He raised one heavy dark eyebrow. 'Hadn't you heard? Beauty is in the eye of the beholder. If I think you're beautiful, then you are. It's a purely subjective judgement. But then I'm partial to women with character.'

'And you think I have character? Whatever that is.'

'Oh, absolutely,' he said with conviction. 'When you say something, you mean it. Much to my regret,' he added ruefully.

His gaze softened then, and the flickering candle on their table caught the dark flecks in his eyes, making them seem almost black. From the background came the soft tinkling of a piano, the low hum of subdued conversation, and Felicia could feel herself gradually being drawn under the hypnotic spell of the romantic atmosphere, the man himself.

The waiter appeared just then to take their dinner order, and, dropping her eyes, she took a quick swallow of her drink. Adam ordered for them both and chose the wine in his usual authoritative tone, and she only nodded when he glanced at her for approval.

'I enjoyed meeting your family at the Bakers' last month,' he said when the waiter had left.

Taken a little off balance by the abrupt change of mood and subject, Felicia told him, 'They enjoyed meeting you too.'

'I'm glad to hear that. How are they? Tell me about them.'

She eyed him warily. 'You're not really interested in my family, are you? We're really all quite dull compared to the exalted circles you travel in.'

'Why, you little snob!' he said in a low voice. 'How do you know what kind of circles I travel in?' He shook his head sadly. 'You know, Felicia, you really should try to overcome your tendency to make snap decisions with very little evidence.'

She raised her chin and gave him a defiant look. 'What about the Courtneys? The Bakers themselves? And prima ballerinas,' she added wickedly.

Adam only raised an eyebrow and gave her a thin smile. 'Are you going to hold that against me the rest of our lives?' he asked pleasantly.

'The rest of our lives?' she asked, laughing. 'What

are you planning to do, adopt me?'

The dark eyes gleamed. 'Maybe. We'll see. Now, let's quit this ridiculous fencing around and just do what I asked you to do. Tell me about your family.'

'All right,' she said, 'you asked for it.'

The waiter came with their dinner, and in between bites she went on to describe what it was like growing up in a doctor's household, the tribulations of being the only girl in a family of three boys, the arguments that escalated at times into physical combat, the close bonds between them all. As she warmed to her subject, describing the idiosyncrasies of each family member, a vivid picture of them all rose up in her mind, so that they almost seemed present in the flesh.

Adam listened to her carefully, without speaking, all through the veal Marsala, and when she finally ran down, he stared at her for some moments, then slowly shook his head from side to side.

'I can't even conceive living like that.'

'Does it sound so awful?' she asked. By now she was painfully aware that she'd been babbling all through dinner, and mentally comparing the rough-and-tumble of her childhood with his own austere upbringing.

'I'm not sure,' he said with a distant look. 'In a way, I envy you.' He lifted his broad shoulders. 'Such a way of life is so utterly foreign to my experience that I have no way to judge.'

'Well, I guess you don't miss what you've never had.'

He mulled this over carefully as he finished his veal and took a long swallow of wine. 'I don't know if that's an entirely accurate statement,' he said thoughtfully. 'Sometimes . . .' His voice trailed off, and he smiled. 'Would you care for some dessert?'

By the time they had left the restaurant and the doorman had whistled down a cab for them, all Felicia's earlier reservations about him had disappeared. Everything about the evening had been so enjoyable that she hated to see it end.

When the taxi pulled up to the kerb, Adam opened the door and helped her inside, then leaned down to speak to the driver, giving him an address on Central Park West. She clamped her jaw shut and gathered up her defences again.

She might have known, she thought bitterly. He was just like all the rest. Wine her and dine her, then take her to his place for the grand seduction scene. The pleasant glow evaporated, and she began to gather all her defences against him.

'I thought you might like to see where I live,' Adam explained as he got in beside her.

He took one look at her, then shook his head ruefully and leaned forward to give the driver her own address.

'Sorry,' he said, as the cab drove off and he settled back in the seat. 'I guess that wasn't such a good idea.'

It all happened so fast that Felicia didn't know now what to think. He had just startled her, that was all. Had it been a perfectly innocent invitation? And was it possible that she was just a little disappointed that he had been so quick to read her unspoken thoughts and had acted on them without any argument?

They rode the rest of the way in silence, and when

they arrived at her building, Adam paid off the cabby, then took her by the arm and walked with her towards the entrance.

'I'll go up with you,' he said. 'I can get another cab later.' He looked up at the clear night sky. 'I might even walk, it's such a nice evening.'

'Yes, it is,' she replied in a stilted tone.

At her door, she turned to face him. He was standing silently at her side, his hands in his pockets, his chin slightly lifted to reveal that wonderful angle of jaw.

'Well,' she said, 'thank you for the dinner.'

Adam smiled and dipped his head. 'My pleasure.'

'Well, goodnight, then,' she said.

He leaned his shoulder up against the wall and looked down at her through half-closed eyes. 'Since you refuse to come to my place, won't you at least give me a drink?'

His voice was low and coaxing, the expression on his face warmly inviting, and for a moment Felicia was tempted. He'd been so nice about everything and she didn't want to antagonise him—at least, not until the bust was finished. But she still sensed danger emanating from him in almost palpable waves.

In a careful voice she said, 'I don't think that would be wise, Adam.'

'Then I guess I'll have to kiss you in the hall,' he said without a moment's hesitation.

He straightened up and a long arm shot out to wind around her neck. She felt herself being propelled forward, enveloped in a close embrace, and then his mouth came down on hers in a gentle, feathery kiss, so unthreatening, so innocent, that she relaxed and allowed herself to lean against him.

'Mm,' he murmured against her lips, 'that's better.'

His mouth opened slightly then, deepening the kiss, and his hands began to stroke slowly up and down over her back, from her waist to her shouders. Her heart began to thud loudly, and a delicious warmth washed over her. But when the hands slid forwards to glide over her ribcage, his thumbs brushing the sides of her breasts, she pulled her head back sharply.

Immediately Adam dropped his hands and moved away from her. 'That was nice,' he said. He took another step back, smiled, and raised a hand to her in a sort of salute. 'I guess I'd better be on my way now. Goodnight, Felicia.'

She looked after him for a moment, then slipped inside her apartment and stood there listening to his footsteps falling away down the hall. In a moment she felt Felix rubbing up against her legs, and stooped down to pick him up, then crossed over to the window. Down on the street, a taxi had just pulled up to the kerb, and she watched as Adam got inside and it drove away. He had certainly given up without a struggle! Perhaps he was angry. She wondered if she would ever see him again, or, more to the point, if she even wanted to see him again.

A dangerous man, she thought as she turned from the window. And, in spite of her desire to finish the statue, her instinct told her that for her sake it would be better, and far safer, if he disappeared out of her life entirely.

On the following Monday, the next regular day for

his sitting, Adam didn't show up at his regular time. Felicia hadn't really expected him, since she'd told him she wouldn't need him any more on a regular basis, yet when one o'clock rolled around, she still listened for his step in the hall, his familiar knock on the door.

She continued working on the head without him, but by Thursday she had reached a point where she would have given a great deal to have him there before her. She couldn't quite get that angle of jaw she wanted, and time after time she'd had to start all over again.

Another week went by. By now she'd begun to suspect that the real reason for his long silence was personal. He'd been very understanding that last night, backing off the second he'd sensed her hesitation about going to his place or deepening that kiss, but he couldn't have liked it. She'd finally given up and turned to her ballerina figurines, but it wasn't the same, and every time she glanced at the half-finished bust, she felt a twinge of regret.

Finally she decided to call him. She fished out the card he had given her and dialled the number. After a few rings, a woman's voice answered. 'St John Enterprises,' came the clipped voice.

'May I speak to Mr St John, please?'

'I'm sorry, he's out of the country. May I take a message?'

Should she or shouldn't she? Well, she wanted to finish the head, didn't she? And for that, she needed him here. 'Yes, please,' she said at last. 'Would you tell him Felicia Fairleigh called?'

Well, that's that, she thought, after she hung up.

Might as well forget it. He wouldn't ever call her again.

The very next afternoon, however, he did call. It was a depressing, grey, drizzly day, but when Felicia heard his voice, it was as though the sun had come out again.

'How's the work going?' he asked. His voice was perfectly normal, just as though nothing had ever happened.

'I'm rather at a standstill at the moment,' she said.

'What seems to be the problem?'

'Well, to tell you the truth, I really could use another sitting, if you have the time. A short one, whenever it's convenient for you.'

'I'll be right over,' Adam said promptly.

'You mean now?'

'Sure. Unless you have other plans.'

'No—no, nothing. That would be wonderful.'

'See you in about half an hour, then,' he said. 'I just came home from the airport a few minutes ago, and I'd like to clean up.'

After she had rung off, she looked around her messy apartment, and immediately began to race around straightening it up. While she was working she rarely paid attention to how the place looked, or even what she'd eaten. Or how she looked either, she thought in a sudden panic as she finished stacking the magazines in a neat pile on the coffee-table.

She flew into the bathroom for a quick shower, hoping she could find her hair-dryer in time, and it wasn't until she was towelling off that she stopped for a moment to consider what she'd been doing for the past fifteen minutes. She stared at her reflection in the bathroom mirror.

'Are you crazy?' she said aloud. The man was coming for a sitting, not a romantic evening. What had got into her? She never behaved like this with men.

She ended by pinning up her hair in its usual casual style and putting on a clean pair of worn jeans and a cotton shirt, and was just getting into her smock when she heard Adam's knock. As she crossed over to the door to let him in, she deliberately made herself walk slowly. She would be businesslike, she told herself calmly. It would be a short session, and then he would go.

By the time she opened the door to him, she was half angry at *him*, as though somehow it was his fault that she had worked herself up so childishly before, and when she spoke to him she put a touch of frost in her voice.

'How are you, Adam?' she said briskly.

'Quite well,' he said, stepping inside. 'And you?'

'Fine. Just fine.' She closed the door and turned to face him. 'Well, shall we get to work?' she asked with a bright, professional smile, and started to lead the way into the studio. 'I really appreciate your coming over like this on such short notice.'

'Not at all,' said Adam in a dry, polite tone. 'I knew that nothing short of a major catastrophe would have induced you to call.'

Ignoring the sarcasm, Felicia crossed over to her work table while he took his usual chair. After she had carefully unwrapped the damp cloths from the clay model, she stared at him for a long time, trying to discover what she'd been getting wrong.

'Could you turn just slightly towards me?' she asked.

'Like this?' He moved his head a few inches in her direction.

She frowned, squinting a little. It still wasn't right. She crossed over to him, hesitated for just a second, then put her hands on his face. His skin felt warm to her touch, and the light stubble on his jaw rasped against her fingers. As she tilted his head slowly she gradually became aware that his eyes were firmly fastened on her, and she drew her hands away as though they had been burned.

Just then she felt herself being lifted bodily off her feet and pulled down into his lap. His arms came around her, cradling her, and his head bent slowly down towards her.

For one second she was tempted, but in the next she froze. 'No,' she said firmly, meeting his eyes at last.

Adam only smiled and kept coming, but just before his mouth made contact she twisted her head to one side. She could sense his hesitation and turned back to face him.

'Adam,' she said quietly, 'you promised you wouldn't do this until the head was finished. Now, please let me go.'

He only held her closer, nuzzling gently just below her ear. 'You said you were almost done.'

Felicia didn't at all like the way his soft mouth was making her feel, and laying her hands flat on his chest, she pushed at him. 'Please stop,' she said shakily.

'Oh, come on, Felicia.' He grabbed at her hands and forced them away from his chest. 'Why do you fight it? We'd be so good together; I promise.'

Irritation began to rise up in her now, and she yanked her hands forcibly out of his grasp. 'What does it take to make you understand?' she breathed angrily. 'I am not interested in playing games with you, Adam. That's not my style at all. I've tried my best to make you see that, but you just won't listen to me.'

'I don't believe you,' he said flatly. 'You're lying.'

But he did release his hold on her. She slid off his lap and walked quickly back to her work table, bracing her hands on the edge and leaning over it, trying to clear her whirling head.

As she stood there, some sixth sense, an imperceptible quickening of her heartbeat, told her Adam was coming up behind her, slowly, soundlessly. She stood transfixed, not moving a muscle, waiting, until she felt his warm breath on the back of her neck.

Then she heard his voice in her ear. 'Let me make love to you, Felicia,' he breathed. 'I've been patient. I haven't pushed. I've tried to respect your wishes all through these damned sittings, and wait until they were finally over. And what's more, you know you want me too.'

Once again she was tempted, but then his last words rang a bell in her mind. Kevin had said much the same thing to her the one and only time she had gone to bed with him. And they had been engaged at the time. This man was a virtual stranger, a man without any feeling for her, who only saw her as another conquest.

She turned around and looked directly into his eyes. 'I said no,' she pronounced firmly, 'and I meant it.'

For several moments he just stood and stared at her. Then he shook his head and ran a hand over his dark hair.

'What is it, Felicia?' he asked in a puzzled tone. 'What's wrong? I know damn well you've enjoyed it the few times you've allowed yourself to respond to me. You can't hide that. Why do you insist on fighting it?'

'You're wrong. Just because I let you kiss me once, it doesn't mean a thing.' She raised her chin. 'I'd like you to leave now,' she added quietly.

Adam flushed deeply at that and frowned at her. 'What the hell is wrong?' he asked in a tight voice.

'Nothing is wrong—except possibly your manners. I'd just like you to leave.'

He continued to stand there glaring at her for a few more seconds, then suddenly his whole body seemed to relax. He gave her a thin, mocking smile. 'No, you wouldn't. You're lying to me again.'

'What makes you think that?' she asked. 'Why do you imagine that every woman is panting after you?'

'I don't,' he said promptly. 'And believe me, I'm not panting after every woman either.' He shrugged. 'But on the other hand, you can't deny the chemistry between us.'

Felicia opened her eyes wide. 'Oh, can't I? I think that's entirely my decision.'

'All right, then. Do you deny it? Swear to me you're not attracted to me as much as I am to you, and I'll promise never to touch you again.'

When she didn't reply, a look of intense satisfaction spread across his face. He cocked an eyebrow and gave her a complacent grin. 'You see?' he asked pleasantly.

'What I feel for you is entirely beside the point,' she said sharply, 'since I have no intention of doing anything about it.'

'That's a pretty perverse position, don't you think?'

'Not at all. It's my choice, and you'll just have to accept it.'

As she watched him, the pleasant smile faded. He dropped his eyes and stared down at the floor, frowning in concentration. He turned from her then, and walked away, his head down, his hands shoved in his trousers pockets jingling keys and change. He moved aimlessly about the room for several moments, then finally came back to face her again.

'How would it be,' he said slowly and carefully, 'if I sweeten the pot a little?'

'What do you mean?' she asked warily.

He gave her a long, quizzical look, then said, 'Laura, at the gallery, tells me you and she have discussed a one-woman show.'

'That's right.'

'She's not sure you're ready.'

'I see,' she said tightly. 'Isn't that her decision?'

His eyes never leaving her face, Adam said softly, 'Yes, but I do have some influence.'

Slowly the light began to dawn. Felicia went hot, then cold, then gave him a narrow-eyed look. 'Let me be quite sure I understand you,' she said carefully, when she was able to speak. 'Are you suggesting that if I agree to a—a closer personal relationship with you, you'll arrange a one-woman show for me at the gallery?'

He shrugged. 'Something like that.'

She gazed at him in horror. 'You mean you want to *buy* me!' she exclaimed.

'Well now, that's putting it a little crudely. I wouldn't do it if I didn't think you were ready for it. I'm a businessman, remember? It would be a mutually profitable venture.' Adam smiled. 'Let's just say I'd be willing to speed up the career that I know is going to succeed anyway, in exchange for . . .'

'Sleeping with you,' she broke in. She drew herself up to her full height, crossed her arms in front of her and looked him up and down severely. 'I'm surprised at you, Adam,' she said with a shake of her head.

He ran a hand over the back of his neck and frowned at her. 'I really don't care at all for the way you put things,' he said. 'If you don't want a one-woman show, why don't you just come out and say so?'

'Of course I want a one-woman show!' she cried. 'But not that way, not with strings like that attached.'

'All right, then!' he shouted angrily. 'You can have the damn show for free. I was only trying to demonstrate my good will.'

'Let me be clear about this, Adam. Are you saying that you'll give me a one-woman show with no strings attached?'

'Yes, that's exactly what I'm saying.'

'I don't believe you,' she stated flatly.

He made a valiant effort to look hurt and indignant, but couldn't quite sustain the effort, and after a few moments of it he smiled thinly. 'Ungrateful little beast, aren't you?'

Felicia raised her chin. 'No, I'm not. I'm just a little too old to believe in fairy-tales, that's all.' She turned from him and started to walk away, feeling rather pleased with the point she had scored, but his arm shot out and held her back. 'Adam,' she said with a sigh, 'please don't start that again.'

He placed both hands on her shoulders and pulled her around bodily to face him. He glared down at her for a long time, a look of intense exasperation on his face, then he sighed deeply.

'For God's sake, Felicia,' he ground out, 'what do I have to do to get you in bed? Marry you?'

She started to laugh, but in the next second a wicked thought popped into her head, an outrageous idea that couldn't possibly work. But it just might put an end to Adam's insistent demands. What she wanted was to finish the statue, and to do that, she had to find a way to keep Adam at a distance and to stay on good terms with him. What better way to do this than to call his bluff?

'Yes,' she said in a firm, ringing tone, 'that's what you'd have to do.'

For a moment Adam only stared at her, obviously thrown off balance by her unequivocal statement. Frowning, he reached up to scratch his head. He gazed pensively off in the distance for a few moments, then turned back to her, his features calm and set.

'All right,' he said. 'If that's what it takes, I'll marry you.'

Felicia stared at him. 'You're crazy!'

'What makes you think so?' he asked in a conversational tone.

She spread her hands helplessly. 'Well, people don't get married for a silly reason like that.'

'Oh, don't they?' he asked grimly. 'I happen to think it's probably the *only* reason people get married at all. What other reason could there possibly be, aside from a masochistic impulse?'

She gave a short laugh. 'I can see you don't have much faith in wedded bliss,' she said drily.

'None at all,' was the cheerful reply.

She shook her head. 'Yet you're willing to marry me?'

'That's right.'

'And how long is this wonderful state of affairs supposed to last?'

Adam shrugged. 'Who knows? As long as we enjoyed each other, I suppose. Don't ask me. It's never crossed my mind before to do such a thing.' He paused for a moment, then looked down at his feet. 'Besides,' he added in an almost inaudible murmur, 'I rather like the idea. Maybe it's time I settled down.'

He was serious, she was finally convinced of that, and she was snared in her own net. Of course, she couldn't possibly marry him. But even as she thought it, that outrageous little idea she'd had a moment ago began to develop into a sneaky plan.

If any man needed teaching a lesson, it was Adam St John. Felicia gave him a cool, appraising look. What she wouldn't give to wipe that smug, arrogant grin off his face! She could just see the wheels turning in that marvellous head. He would marry her, use her sexually until he was tired of her and wanted to go on to greener pastures, then obtain a divorce, so quick and easy these days.

He didn't have the slightest notion that marriage meant love, commitment, responsibility, caring, building a life, even children. He quite simply wanted what he wanted, and was even willing to go this far to get it.

As the plan ripened in her mind, she became filled with a heady sense of power. If it worked—and there was no reason why it shouldn't—she would be dealing a blow for all of womankind. To outwit this overbearing, conceited man once and for all would be worth all the trouble she'd have to go through to do it.

'All right,' she said, 'I'll marry you.'

Although she could have sworn Adam was momentarily nonplussed, he recovered himself instantly. 'Good,' he said, and began to walk slowly towards her, the grey-blue eyes gleaming.

'Not so fast!' she said, stepping back a pace. 'That's not part of the bargain. I said I'd marry you, not hop into bed with you tonight.'

'What's the difference?' he asked with a frown. 'Are you afraid I might welsh on the deal?'

'Well, I don't know that, do I?' she asked pleasantly. 'You might. In any case, the whole point is lost if the wedding ceremony doesn't come first.'

Adam put his hands on his hips and gave her a crooked smile. 'I can see it would be a mistake to underestimate you,' he said softly. Then he nodded. 'All right, we'll do it your way. I make only one condition.'

'What's that?'

'We get married as soon as possible—say next week. I don't believe in long engagements.'

Felicia thought furiously. The head was almost finished. With one more week of sittings, she could complete it without him. It was rushing things a little, but she could see he was quite firm.

'All right,' she said at last, 'I agree. Next week it'll be.'

Adam held out a hand. 'Shall we shake on it?'

CHAPTER SEVEN

WHEN he was gone, Felicia sank down in a chair, still dazed. Married! She could still hardly take it in. Even though it was only to be a parody of a real marriage, it was impossible to believe that Adam actually intended to go through with it.

Yet he had seemed quite determined to do just that, and considering his firmly voiced convictions on the subject she had to wonder why. Was it possible that in his way he really did care about her, actually meant to take the commitment seriously?

She laughed aloud. The thought was ludicrous. In his view, marriage for *any* reason was a joke, and he had agreed so easily for only one reason: he knew it was the only way he would ever get her into his bed. At the thought, a bitter resentment rose within her, almost choking her.

She jumped up and started pacing around the room. Men! They were all alike. But she'd show him! If ever a man needed teaching a lesson, it was Adam St John, and she would fix it so that he *couldn't* back out, even if he did change his mind.

She picked up the telephone and dialled Carol's number. While she listened to it ring, she went over the terms of the odd bargain they had struck, and couldn't recall one word that had committed her to sleep with Adam, even after the ridiculous wedding. If he chose to infer a guarantee on her part to do so, that was his lookout, but she was satisfied that she had made no such promise.

'Hello,' came Carol's voice.

Felicia drew in a deep breath and took the plunge. 'I wanted you to be the first to know, Carol,' she said. 'I'm going to marry Adam St John.'

There was total silence at the other end of the line, then a strangled squawking sound as Carol exploded. 'You're what?' she cried. 'I think we must have a bad connection. Would you repeat that, please?'

Felicia smiled grimly. 'You heard me right the first time. Adam has asked me to marry him, and I told him I would.'

'I don't believe it. I simply don't believe it!'

'What don't you believe?' Felicia asked, highly amused. 'That he wants to marry me, or that I agreed to do it?'

'Well, both, I guess,' came Carol's bewildered voice. 'I mean, I guess I can understand why he wants to marry you, but I was positive you'd never let any man get that close to you again. What in the world happened to change your mind?'

'Let's just say he's irresistible,' Felicia replied drily. 'He swept me off my feet, battered down my resistance, and in the end I just couldn't refuse him.'

'You sound funny,' Carol said in a cautious tone.

'How do you mean, funny?' Actually, it was all Felicia could do to keep from breaking out laughing.

'Not at all like a woman in love, if you want the truth.'

'Well, it only happened tonight. I haven't quite got used to the idea yet.'

'Have you told your parents yet?'

'Not yet.' As a matter of fact, she wasn't too thrilled about the little deception she'd have to practise on them. 'I wanted you to be the first to know.'

Carol giggled. 'Wait until Irina hears! Gossip has it that the real reason she and Adam broke up was that he wouldn't marry her. I've got to hand it to you, Felicia,' she said admiringly, 'you've pulled off a real coup, walked away with one of New York's most elusive prize bachelors.'

Felicia rolled her eyes. 'Oh, he's a real prize, all right.'

'When is it to be?' Carol asked. 'I mean, can I tell people?'

'Oh, yes. Put it in the newspaper if you'd like.' The more public it became, the harder it would be for Adam to back down. 'It'll be some time next week.' As soon as I don't need any more sittings from him, she added to herself.

With more effusive congratulations from Carol, they finally hung up. Then, before she could lose her nerve, Felicia called her parents. If she waited until morning, she was afraid she wouldn't be able to do it at all.

Her mother answered the telephone, and when Felicia told her the news she broke instantly into loud expressions of joy.

'Oh, darling, I'm so happy for you!' she cried ecstatically. 'He's such a nice man, and I know you'll be happy with him. I've been so worried about you, ever since Kevin, and nothing in this world could please me more than to see you happily married to a good man like Adam.'

As she listened to the little catch in her mother's voice, Felicia's feelings of guilt escalated almost out of control. What she planned to do might be considered unsportsmanlike in some quarters, but technically she was only misleading him, not actually deceiving him, and she did balk at doing anything positively immoral.

Finishing the clay mould was the important thing, she thought fiercely, and she had only a week to do it in. Once they were married and she went through with her plan, she had no doubt that it would be the last she'd ever see of him, and she desperately wanted to have the head all ready for casting before then.

It's all in a good cause, she told herself to bolster her flagging determination, and if her mother only knew just how 'good' and 'nice' the man really was, she reasoned, she wouldn't be quite so anxious to see her daughter married to him.

Absorbed in her own thoughts, she only half listened to her mother's euphoric chatter, until she heard her making plans for a June wedding at home. 'Not that I believe in long engagements,' she was going on happily, 'but the garden is so lovely at that time of year, and I've alway wanted . . .'

'Mother,' Felicia interrupted firmly, 'I'm sorry to spoil your plans, but we're not going to wait until June. For heaven's sake, it's not even Christmas yet! We're not starry-eyed children, you know. I'm already twenty-six, and Adam is ten years older.'

After she had soothed her mother about depriving her of a garden wedding in June and hung up the phone, Felicia felt totally wiped out. What a day! she thought, as she fixed the loudly complaining Felix his bedtime snack. And what a week she would have ahead of her!

True to his word, Adam left her alone during the entire week. He sat patiently for her for as long as she required, and while he might accept a cup of coffee or a beer during the short afternoon break, he always left promptly as soon as the day's session was over.

In fact, he kept his distance so faithfully that Felicia began to wonder if the whole thing had been a dream, or if he had changed his mind. In a way, she hoped so. Not only did it bother her to deceive her family and friends by letting them assume it would be a genuine marriage, but now that Adam was behaving himself so beautifully she found herself quite enjoying his company.

By Thursday afternoon, in fact, she had made up her mind to call the whole thing off herself. All the zest seemed to have gone out of it now that her anger at him had cooled. This would be their last session and, as she worked, she decided to tell him she'd changed her mind as soon as she was through.

After another hour's work, she stepped back from the clay model and eyed it critically. It had come right at last, and an intense thrill of satisfaction ran through her at the sight of the work she had created. It had caught exactly the expression she wanted. No more sittings would be necessary.

She glanced at Adam, who raised an eyebrow enquiringly at her. 'Are you finished?' he asked.

She nodded. 'I think so. Do you want to come and look?

He rose from his chair and came to stand by her side, gazing down at the completed head. Then he looked at her. 'It's very good,' he said quietly. 'Very good indeed.' Then he frowned and looked at it again. 'Although it's not really an exact likeness, is it? But then, I guess it's not supposed to be.'

She was a little surprised at his reaction. To her the likeness was quite accurate. She looked from the man to the statue. No, she decided, he was wrong. She had captured the essence of Adam St John in clay exactly as she had pictured him.

'Don't you like it?' she asked at last.

'Oh, yes,' he assured her hurriedly, 'I like it very much.' He stretched widely then and smiled down at her. 'I'm also very glad to have it over and done with.' He reached out and put his hands on her shoulders. 'Now we can get on to more important things. We have a wedding tomorrow, remember?'

As his hands tightened, Felicia thought, I've got to tell him now. She gave him a hesitant look. 'Adam,' she began, 'about the wedding . . .' She paused, searching for the right words.

'What is it? Have you changed your mind and decided to invite your parents, after all?'

'No, it isn't that.' To her mother's disappointment, Felicia had insisted that they not attend. She simply couldn't face the good wishes of her family and friends when the whole thing was only a farce, a travesty.

'Well, what, then? Don't tell me you've decided you don't want to go to Nassau on our honeymoon? The reservations are all made.' Adam pulled her to him and buried his face in her hair. 'I've been looking forward all week to that honeymoon,' he murmured. 'It's a perfect place, far enough away for privacy, yet close enough to get there in a hurry. And I'm in a hell of a hurry, Felicia.'

She pulled away from him and looked directly into his eyes. 'Adam, I've been thinking—it's wrong for us to get married. I want to call it off.'

His dark eyebrows shot up and he frowned at her. 'Call it off? You can't call it off. We made a bargain. I've fulfilled my part of it, now it's your turn.'

Felicia clasped her hands in front of her and walked away from him to stand at the window. 'Oh, Adam, don't you see? I can't marry you. It would be wrong.'

'It's too late for that,' he said sharply.

She whirled around to face him. 'Just think for a minute,' she pleaded. 'Marriage is a serious business, or it should be. We don't really *care* about each other, and I can't just make a mockery of something that should be a solemn commitment.'

Adam eyed her carefully for a few moments, then said quietly, 'What makes you think I don't care about you? Why else would I be marrying you? What do you think I've been trying to tell you all these weeks?'

'All right,' she admitted, 'I guess, in your way, you do feel something for me, but that's not love, and it certainly isn't enough to base a marriage on.'

He shrugged and averted his eyes. 'I don't know anything about that,' he said distantly. Then he turned back to her and gave her a piercing look. 'I only know I want you badly enough to marry you. Isn't that enough?'

The words were spoken slowly, as though wrung

out of him by a painful effort. A bright flicker of genuine hope rose within her, warming her, and for a moment she was tempted. Was it possible that Adam did love her without realising it? Could she, did she dare, trust him? Enough to give herself to him willingly?

Then she thought of Kevin. She'd fallen into that trap once before, and she wouldn't do it again. 'No,' she said quietly, 'it's not enough, Adam. Not for me.'

His eyes clouded over for a brief moment, then he nodded abruptly. 'All right,' he said in a clipped voice, 'I see your point, and while I don't entertain the same awed reverence you do for matrimony, I agree with you that there's no earthly reason for us to get married. If you recall,' he continued drily, 'it wasn't exactly marriage I had on my mind in the first place. I'm perfectly willing to call the wedding off.'

Felicia heaved a sigh of relief. 'I knew you'd see reason, Adam,' she said gratefully, but when he began to walk slowly towards her, and she saw the determined look in his eye, she shrank back from him.

'What I'm *not* willing to do, however,' he said firmly, 'is let you off your end of our agreement.'

She put a hand at her throat. 'What—what do you mean?'

'I mean, Felicia, that while I don't give a damn one way or the other about marrying you, I have every intention of taking you to bed. That was your promise, and that's what I'm holding you to.'

Clearly he meant exactly what he said, and she knew he wouldn't back down an inch. 'I never promised any such thing,' she said with a lift of her chin.

'That was your idea, not mine.'

'Nice try, Felicia. But you did agree to marry me, and in my book that amounts to the same thing.'

Maybe in your book, she thought as the anger rose up in her, but not in mine. She'd done her best, she decided, tried to talk some sense into him, but obviously he was so bound and determined to get his own way at any price that talk was useless. She'd just have to go through with her plan. It would serve him right!

With a heroic effort she controlled her irritation and gave him a bright smile. 'OK,' she said, 'if that's the way you want it, then I'm afraid we'll have to get married, after all.'

Adam lifted his broad shoulders. 'Fine. As I said, it makes no difference to me one way or the other.'

He took a step towards her, but she moved quickly out of his way. 'Sorry,' she said sweetly. 'We're not married yet, and a bargain is a bargain. Remember?'

It wasn't until he was safely out of the door and she was quite sure he'd gone that Felicia let herself go. With a low cry of sheer disgust, she began pacing back and forth throughout the whole apartment, wringing her hands and cursing the man she was going to marry tomorrow.

'Of all the arrogant, bullheaded men in creation,' she muttered under her breath, 'why did he have to barge into my life?'

She strode into the living-room, to see Felix curled up in his favourite chair, eyeing her sombrely. Kneeling down beside him, she stroked his silky coat.

'But we'll show him, old boy. We'll teach Mr Adam Conceited St John a lesson he'll never forget!'

She glanced at her watch. There was still time to carry out her plan, but she'd have to hurry. She jumped to her feet and ran into the bedroom to pick up her handbag. Shopping first, she decided, as she grabbed a jacket out of the wardrobe and slipped into it on her way to the front door. Then, if she could find a place that would take her on such short notice, a new hairstyle, something really obvious, she thought grimly as she ran down the stairs. Something that would transform her into the cheap sex object Adam seemed to find so irresistible. And after that, the travel agency for a return ticket home.

Down in the street, she stuffed her hands in her jacket pocket, hunched herself forward against the chill November wind, and started walking east in the direction of Fifth Avenue.

Late the next afternoon Felicia sat beside her new husband on the plane heading for Miami. The plan was to spend their wedding night at one of the luxury hotels in Miami Beach, then go on the next morning to Nassau in the Bahamas for the rest of their two-week honeymoon.

Her husband! She could hardly believe she'd really done it, actually gone through with a ceremony that should have been the most serious commitment of her life, but which she viewed now as only a move in the complex game she was playing with this man.

So far her plan had worked perfectly. Last night's shopping expedition had paid off handsomely, and Adam didn't appear to be in the least suspicious. Naturally not, she thought wryly. With an ego like his, he would automatically assume the transformation in her appearance and the general softening in her attitude towards him were entirely due to the mad, uncontrollable passion he was so convinced she harboured for him.

She had chosen the slinky white dress with care. It had been outrageously expensive, but worth every penny, she decided, when she'd seen the way his eyes had swept appreciatively over her at the sight of it that afternoon at the Court House. It was a clinging silk jersey that hugged every curve of her slim body.

As an added touch, to further whet his appetite, Felicia had gone braless. Although her breasts were high and firm, the thin material left little to the imagination, and the revealing surplice bodice was cut so low in front that all she had to do was lean over in a certain way to reveal a good portion of cleavage.

A new hairstyle completed the picture. The sleek upsweep in the back and clever cut of the fringe at her forehead and around her ears gave her a warm, tumbled look, and the blonde rinse highlighted the streaks in her long honey-coloured hair.

The girl at the beauty shop had shown her how to use a greenish shadow that made her hazel eyes look huge, and she had practised batting them suggestively in the mirror until she was certain she had the look down perfectly—sexy, but not blatantly so.

Adam had been very quiet all afternoon. After that one rather startled look when he'd first seen her in her 'disguise', he'd hardly said a word while they waited their turn at the Court House to be married. He had sat beside her on the bench outside the Judge's chambers, smoking silently, his expression thoughtful.

After the short, impersonal ceremony before Judge Whittaker, who was an old friend of Adam's family, he had kissed her very briefly, his lips cool and dry, and they had ridden out to the airport on Long Island in almost total silence.

Felicia glanced at him now out of the corner of her eye. His head was resting back against his seat and turned in her direction, and he was staring at her through half-closed eyes. As their eyes met, she felt a sharp pang of conscience at what she was doing. In spite of his arrogance, he was a likeable man, and she still found his physical good looks most compelling.

She had awakened that morning with a splitting headache that was still with her. Guilt, she supposed, and had seriously considered calling the whole thing off. But it was too late for that.

Adam shifted slightly in his seat and reached over to take her hand. It was growing dark outside, and the lights in the cabin had not yet been turned on, but there was no mistaking the gleam that deepened his blue-grey eyes.

When he leaned closer to her, letting his hand rest on her thigh, his touch seemed to burn right through the thin white material. Felicia drew in a deep inward breath, and once again steeled herself against him. She had to go through with it now. Anything else was unthinkable.

'Well,' he said in a low, intimate tone, 'how does it feel to be Mrs St John?'

Her first impulse was to brush away the large, well-shaped hand that was moving now up and down her thigh, and her second to tell him in no uncertain terms that her name was not Mrs Anybody, it was Felicia Fairleigh, now and for ever. Instead, she gritted her teeth and cocked an eyebrow at him.

'I don't know yet,' she purred throatily. 'Ask me tomorrow.'

'I'll do that,' said Adam, his eyes burning into hers.

His fingers were inching slowly upwards, and she shifted uncomfortably in her seat. Suppressing a frown and pouting prettily, she put her hand on top of his.

'Adam,' she said playfully, 'there are people all around. Can't you wait?'

He shook his dark head. 'I'll try,' he said, sighing heavily and slowly, reluctantly drawing his hand away, 'but it won't be easy.'

'Don't you know that deferring a pleasure makes it even more enjoyable when you finally get it?' she asked lightly.

He moved away from her and settled back in his seat. 'You may be right,' he said, giving her a long look full of meaning, 'but this is one pleasure that's been deferred for far too long.'

He leaned his head back again and closed his eyes, and Felicia breathed a sigh of relief. Another hurdle passed.

At the hotel, as she waited for Adam to register, she had her first serious crisis of nerves. The really tricky part was still ahead of her. She stood to one side, watching him as he spoke to the desk clerk in his low, authoritative tone, and tried to work up some of her old resentment towards him.

'That's right,' he was saying, 'Mr and Mrs Adam St

John. My secretary made the reservations a week ago,' and when he turned to smile at Felicia, she wondered if she was quite sure she *wanted* to go through with it. If only he weren't so appealing! If only he weren't so nice! In her heart of hearts, she knew she wanted him to make love to her. Even though there was no possible future with him, it would be an experience to look back on for the rest of her life.

There was something about Miami, too, something about the balmy salt air, the soft, warm evening breeze. It was an ideal spot for a real honeymoon. The wide, palm-lined streets and stretches of white sandy beach were all such a stark contrast to the crowds and pollution and traffic of New York, which was now in the first chilly grip of wintry weather.

Adam was walking towards her now in his easy, graceful gait, looking marvellous, so tall and handsome with his dark head and fine features. He had worn a dark grey suit with a lighter pearl-grey waistcoat and white shirt, and he was by far the most impressive-looking man in the hotel lobby. If only . . .

'Would you like a drink before we go up?' he asked. 'Are you hungry?'

'Not really,' Felicia said weakly.

'All right, then,' he said, taking her lightly by the elbow, 'let's go.' The hand on her arm tightened as he guided her forwards, and he leaned down to murmur in her ear, 'We can have something sent up—later.'

They rode up to the top floor in silence. Leave it to Adam, Felicia thought as they glided upwards, to choose the most expensive suite just for one night!

Not even one night, she reassured herself, clutching tightly at her handbag. Inside were her reservation and return ticket on the ten o'clock flight back to New York that night.

The bellboy unlocked the door and they stepped inside the large suite. She stood and stared at the beautifully furnished sitting-room, one wall of which was entirely made of glass and which overlooked the beach. While the boy took their bags into the adjoining bedroom, she walked around the lovely room, examining everything, until she came to the window and stood gazing out at the phosphorescent surf, twenty storeys below.

There was a full moon in the midnight-blue sky, which was clear as a bell and dotted with twinkling stars. From the wide terrace just below at the edge of the beach came the sounds of laughter, an orchestra playing, and the scent of jasmine was heavy on the soft evening air.

Once again Felicia felt a pang of regret that this wasn't going to be a real honeymoon. Everything—the setting, the lovely suite of rooms, even the man himself—spelled romance.

The bellboy was leaving now, and it was time to begin. While Adam attended to him at the door, she set her bag down on the wide, upholstered couch and went into the bedroom. There was a desk, a dresser and, dominating the room, a large king-sized bed, covered with a rich plum-coloured satin spread.

She stared at it for a moment, then turned quickly to examine the adjoining bath, a huge room with pale pink-tiled walls, a thickly carpeted floor and marble fixtures. Plummy towels and washcloths hung on the racks, and there was room enough in the large oval tub for at least three people.

Felicia went back into the bedroom and opened her suitcase. All it contained were the suit and blouse she would wear on the plane back to New York, and the nightgown she had bought as a prop for the little drama she was staging. She lifted it carefully out of the layers of tissue paper and stared at it. She had almost been embarrassed to buy it in the first place, and even now her face flushed as she gazed down at the gossamer concoction of sheerest skin-coloured silk and lace.

She heard the bellboy leaving in the next room, and quickly laid the nightgown down on top of the bed, arranging it so that it showed to full advantage. Then, a few moments later, she turned to see Adam standing in the doorway. Her heart started pounding uncontrollably, her knees felt weak, and it was all she could do to keep from reaching out to the nearby bedpost for support.

She had a sudden, overpowering urge to tell him that the whole thing was a terrible mistake, to simply grab her suitcase and run, but she knew it was too late. As he began to walk slowly towards her, her eyes seemed to widen further wth each step he took, and she had to resist the impulse to back away from him.

When he reached her, he glanced down at the wicked nightgown lying on the bed, then turned to gaze at her for some moments, his eyes alight with anticipation. Felicia waited, breathless. Her timing had to be just right. Too soon, and he'd get suspicious, too late, and she wouldn't stand a chance.

'Now,' he said at last in a tone of intense satisfaction. 'Now it's your turn to fulfil your part of our bargain.'

CHAPTER EIGHT

AS ADAM reached out for her, she closed her eyes and allowed him to take her into his arms. His breath was warm at her ear. 'You won't regret it, Felicia,' he murmured. 'I'm going to make this a night you'll never forget.'

He bent his head and placed his lips on hers in a soft, sensuous kiss. She had expected him to take her swiftly, suddenly, and this slow, gentle pressure of his mobile mouth filled her with a pleasurable warm glow that seemed to penetrate to the very marrow of her bones.

She hadn't counted on this. What was happening to her? She couldn't think. She was having trouble remembering her plan, something about getting him out of the suite so that she could leave for the airport when he was gone. Now the details were getting fuzzier with each passing moment. If only her head would stop that awful pounding!

She tried to remember what kind of man Adam was. He didn't love her; he had married her only to get her into bed. When he had tired of her, he'd leave her. But somehow all that didn't seem quite so important now, as his mouth opened wider and his tongue pushed past her lips, deepening the kiss.

His hands began to glide slowly up and down her back, from her shoulders to her hips, the silky material of her dress slithering sensually over the bare skin underneath. As he moulded her body all along the hard length of him, it seemed to her that they were melting together, fusing into one person.

After a while, he drew his head back and gazed directly into her eyes for several moments. Felicia felt she was drowning in those blue-grey eyes, softer now than she had ever seen them before, and gleaming with the light of desire. It was then, in a sudden burst of clarity, that she knew she couldn't deceive him the way she'd planned. Not only because she had made the bargain and he trusted her to go through with it, nor even that it was flattering to be so ardently desired.

She wanted him! There was no denying it now. She had always wanted him, from the first moment she'd noticed his wonderful head after that dreadful ballet, when she'd tripped over his feet. It didn't matter that he had no intention of making this a real marriage or that he didn't love her or that she would only be repeating what she had gone through with Kevin. None of that mattered now. All she knew was that it was heaven to be in his arms, to know that she was the one who could light up his eyes that way.

Still holding her gaze in his, he slid his hands slowly down from her shoulders now, to rest over her breasts. The shock of that warm, intimate touch shot through her like an electric current.

'I've waited a long time for this, Felicia,' he murmured, pressing her lower body up against his, so that she could feel the hard evidence of his own desire thrusting against her.

She stood before him, rooted to the spot, unable to move, and watched as he lowered one hand to loosen the fastening of the dress at her waist. He pushed aside the opening of the bodice so that her breasts were half exposed, then slipped his hands under the material, where they continued to work their magic in sure, expert strokes, warm and gentle on her bare skin.

'God, how I want you!' he breathed, and tugged the dress over her shoulders, pulling it down over her arms until it hung loosely around her waist.

For a long, tense moment, he stared fixedly at her bare breasts, high and firm; then, with a little noise deep in his throat, he jerked his head back and stepped a pace away from her. Felicia watched him, hardly able to breathe, as he loosened his tie, pulled it over his head, then slowly unbuttoned his shirt and tore it off, to reveal the broad, muscled expanse of his tanned chest.

When he reached for her again, she closed her eyes and let her head fall back, as his hungry mouth descended to her breast. She had never before in her life experienced the sensations he was awakening in her, never known the piercing agony, half pain, half pleasure, of such intense desire. She reached out blindly to put her hands on his head, the crisp black hair springy under her fingers.

All of a sudden her head began to swim with an ominous numbing sensation, and a buzzing sound filled her ears. Her throat seemed to have dried up, and she swallowed convulsively. 'Adam . . .' she murmured as her knees gave way. Then blackness descended, and she was falling, falling . . .

She was inside a dark tunnel. Someone was holding her hands, chafing her wrists, and from a great distance she heard a man's voice calling to her.

'Felicia, wake up! Darling, are you all right? Come on, love, speak to me!'

When she opened her eyes again, she was lying down, her dress back in place. Blinking, she looked up to see that Adam was sitting beside her on the bed, bending over her, his features drawn, his face white with concern.

'Adam?' she said weakly.

'Thank God!' he breathed, and leaned over to kiss her forehead.

'What happened?'

His expression was still gave. 'You passed out, that's what happened.'

There was still a dull ache at the back of her head, and she didn't dare move. 'How long have I been out?' she asked.

'Just a few seconds.' He smiled down at her. 'That's the first time I've had that kind of reaction to my lovemaking!'

Felicia shook her head to clear it, and immediately a blinding shaft of pain ran through it. With a groan, she turned her head on the pillows and closed her eyes, but in the next moment she felt the bed shift with Adam's movement, and opened them again to see that Adam was striding purposefully towards the door into the sitting-room.

'Where are you going?' she called after him.

'I'll be right back. I'm going to call a doctor,' was the firm reply.

She rose up on one elbow. 'No, don't do that please! I'll be all right.' He gave her a dubious look. 'Honestly,' she said. She forced out a laugh, hoping to allay his concern. 'It's been a long day, and I haven't eaten anything since breakfast. Really, I'm fine now.'

He walked slowly back to the bed and stood over it, looking down at her. 'You're sure?'

She smiled up at him. 'Honestly.' She raised herself up and swung her legs over the side of the bed. 'It's only a headache. I have some aspirin in my handbag, that will fix me up just fine.'

Adam leaned over, took her firmly by the shoulders and forced her gently back down on the bed. 'I'll get the aspirin. I'm going to call room service and have them send up something to eat anyway. You stay right where you are. Don't even think of getting up.'

'Yes, sir,' she said meekly.

As she watched him walk away from her, she marvelled once again at the beauty of his body, the wide, muscled shoulders, the strong, tanned back that tapered down to narrow hips, where the trousers to his suit were slung low. He was concerned about her, she thought happily. He really seemed to care.

It wasn't until he had disappeared and she heard him in the other room that it dawned on her. The ticket home! It was still in her bag! When Adam opened it to get the aspirin he would see it. She leaped out of bed, ignoring her throbbing head, and stumbled to the door into the sitting-room.

When she got there, he was standing by the couch, staring down at the open bag in his hands, a puzzled frown on his face. Felicia's heart sank. It was too late. Slowly he took out the telltale envelope, opened it, then raised his head and looked at her.

'What's this?' he asked in a low voice.

She didn't know what to say, but the one thing she knew she couldn't do was lie to him. Somehow she had to make him understand that she had changed her mind, that even though she had been planning to leave him, in the end she had decided to stay, wanted to stay.

He brandished the envelope at her. 'You never intended to go through with it, did you, Felicia?' he asked in a hard, cold voice. 'You had your exit all planned, right from the beginning.'

'Adam—please! Let me explain.'

There was a long silence while he simply stared past her. 'All right,' he said at last, 'Let's hear it.'

She took a step towards him, but the cold, menacing look on his face stopped her. She put a hand to her throat. 'OK—I admit I did plan to leave you tonight.'

Adam raised an eyebrow. 'I see. Tell me, just as a matter of academic interest, had you planned to make your great escape before or after I made love to you?'

Totally unable to face him, she stared down at her hands and started twisting them nervously together. 'Before,' she mumbled.

'Why, Felicia?' he ground out. 'Why did you agree to *marry* me, for God's sake, if you despised me so much you had to sneak out on me practically the minute we got here?' He took a step towards her. 'Why go to all this trouble just to brush me off? Was it really necessary to go to such lengths? To deceive me like this?'

He took another step towards her, and she shrank back, really frightened now. His eyes were like chunks of ice, his face suffused with barely contained rage, and she was certain that in the next moment he would raise his hand and strike her.

Well, she deserved it, she thought miserably. He was standing stock still, not four paces away from her, his hands clenched into fists at his sides, glaring down at her as though she were some specimen of particularly obnoxious insect.

She wanted to crawl into a hole and die. She'd never felt so horribly ashamed of herself in her life. Somehow she had to explain to him, make him understand.

She raised her eyes to his and held out a hand. 'Adam, I know I did wrong, and I'm sorry . . .'

'Sorry?' he shouted. 'God, that's the last straw! You tricked me into a marriage you knew damned good and well I didn't want, you responded to me as though you really meant it, even enjoyed it, and all along this diabolical scheme of yours is in the works!'

At his words, Felicia's guilt and fear gradually faded, and a slow anger began to simmer deep down inside her. He didn't care two pins for her; all he was worried about was his precious ego. She raised her chin and stood her ground.

'I didn't trick you into marriage, Adam,' she said in a low, controlled voice. 'That was your idea, if you remember.'

'It was a bargain,' he said evenly through his tightly clenched teeth.

'All right, it was a bargain. And I would have gone through with it. I honoured my part of it.'

He waved the ticket at her again. 'You call this honouring your bargain?' he exploded.

'I'm still here, aren't I? I didn't do it, did I?' She

crossed her arms in front of her and gave him a scathing look. As she watched him, his eyes dropped away and all the anger seemed to drain out of him. He turned from her to reach for his shirt and tie, still lying on the floor where he'd dropped them not half an hour ago. Slowly he buttoned up the shirt, tucked it inside the waistband of his dark trousers and tightened the tie. Then he retrieved his suit jacket from the chair and walked to the door.

'Your plane leaves in an hour,' he said in a flat, dull voice. 'You can take a cab. Do you need some money?'

'No.'

'All right, then.' He opened the door.

'Where—where are you going?' she faltered.

He turned to her. 'If it matters to you, probably the first thing I'll do is go get drunk.'

He stepped out into the hall and closed the door firmly behind him. Felicia stood there staring blankly at the door for several seconds, then slowly walked over to the telephone to call for a cab.

It only took about ten minutes to get herself pulled together and gather up her suitcase and handbag. When she was through, she went to the door and opened it cautiously, peering out into the hall to make sure Adam was nowhere in sight. She couldn't face him now.

All she saw was a waiter in a white jacket carrying a huge bouquet of red roses. He came towards her, smiling and gazing at her politely.

'Miss Fairleigh?' he asked.

Falicia groaned inwardly. What now? 'Yes,' she said impatiently, edging away from him, 'I'm Felicia Fairleigh.'

'This is for you,' he told her.

She stared blankly at him. 'For me?'

She stared at the bouquet. The flowers were lovely, a deep red, and so heavily perfumed that the scent filled the hallway. She'd never seen so many roses; there must have been at least four dozen in the crystal vase, some full-blown, some still in bud.

'Thank you,' she said hurriedly. She rummaged in her bag, took out a bill and shoved it at him.

'Thank *you*,' he replied. Then he handed her a small envelope. 'The gentleman said to give this to you personally after I delivered the flowers.'

When he was gone, Felicia hurried back inside, set the vase down, then stood staring at the envelope in her hand. Quickly she tore it open. Inside was a single sheet of hotel stationery, covered with a brief message in slashing black ink. Although she'd never seen Adam's handwriting before, she hadn't a doubt in the world that it was his. It suited him somehow, a no-nonsense, supremely self-confident hand that could only belong to a man like him.

The message was brief and to the point:

'My dear Felicia,

A small token of my sincere regret for the way things have turned out, and an apology for whatever part I played in this little fiasco. I also want to assure you that I would never have forced you against your will. It troubles me that you might have thought that.

'Goodbye, and good luck with your work. I won't bother you again.'

It was signed simply, 'Adam.'

Felicia sank down slowly on to the couch as she read,

then she read it again. By then it felt as though the whole top of her head would come off at any moment, and she was limp from the emotions warring within her—shame, guilt, anger, humiliation and, she had to admit, regret, all fought for supremacy in her mind.

Well, she decided at last, one thing was clear. Her little plan had backfired disastrously. Adam had won, after all. It was he who had come out of it making her look like a fool. Nausea began to rise up in her throat, gagging her, and then, along with everything else, the tears began to threaten.

No! she thought fiercely. I won't give in to that. It's too late. All she wanted now was to get out of there and return to the safety of her own comfortable apartment, her work, her plants, Felix, who by now was probably furious at her. She'd gambled and lost, and, like a sensible gambler, she should cut those losses and get on with her life.

Crumpling up the note and stuffing it in her jacket pocket, she jammed the airline ticket in her handbag, picked up her bag, and walked out of the room.

In the days that followed, Felicia did her best to avoid seeing or talking to her friends and family, but a certain amount of it was inevitable.

She parried their dumbfounded enquiries about her solitary return to New York by simply telling them she didn't want to talk about it and flatly refusing to give any explicit reason why she and her new husband had separated only hours after their wedding.

She had made only one feeble attempt at an explanation to Carol, her best friend. When she had arrived back in New York, she felt she had to talk to someone about it, and had called Carol the next day. She shuddered even now, three weeks later, as she recalled that awful conversation.

'You did what?' Carol had shouted to her over the telephone.

'Well, he needed teaching a lesson,' Felicia had replied defensively.

After that, there was no stopping Carol. 'I don't believe you. What did Adam ever do to you to make you treat him like that? How has he ever harmed you? My God, girl, he pursued you, he wanted you, he showed you in every possible way how much he cared about you, even to the point of marrying you. What more do you want? What's wrong with you?'

'Well, thanks a lot,' Felicia had retorted glumly. 'You're making me feel a lot better!'

'You don't *deserve* to feel better! You've hurt that man in the worst possible way a woman could, and I have no sympathy for you whatsoever.'

'Listen, Carol, I'm trying to tell you. The marriage was only a farce to begin with. He never meant anything serious by it or intended it to be lasting. Believe me, I'm well out of it. He would have left me eventually, when he was tired of me. He's no different from all the rest, just like . . .'

'Just like Kevin,' Carol broke in. Then she sighed deeply. 'You thought it was Kevin all over again, I understand that. But you're wrong this time, Felicia—dead wrong.'

Troubled by Carol's scathing indictment of her, Felicia did what she swore she would never do and went on to tell her the whole truth. 'Well, if it makes you feel any better, I'd already changed my mind. If he hadn't found that ticket, everything would have turned out quite differently.'

There was a long silence. Then Carol sighed and said, 'I'm sorry about that, Felicia, really I am. Is there no hope at all that you can explain things to him, get back together? After all, you *are* married to the man.'

Felicia gave a bitter laugh. 'Afraid not. In the mood Adam was in after he found that ticket, I have no doubt whatsoever he found consolation for his wounded ego somewhere else in short order.'

That conversation had been the beginning and the end of her attempts to explain to *anyone* what had really happened. She didn't know about Adam, but for her part she intended to keep silence to the grave on the subject from then on.

The one bright spot in those terrible days was a telephone call from Laura at the gallery in mid-November, about a week after her ignominious flight from Miami.

'How would you like that one-woman show we talked about some weeks ago?' was her opening question.

'Well, I'd love it, of course,' Felicia replied slowly. 'But why me?'

'Because I think you're ready for it, of course,' was the brisk reply. 'I'd like you to gather together as much of your work as you can. Do you think you could be ready by late December? I thought the week before Christmas might be the best time. Catch the last-minute shoppers, you know.'

Felicia hesitated. She wanted that one-woman show badly. It would be a tremendous boost to her badly damaged ego at this point, and a real step up in her career. But she couldn't do it if Adam were to be involved in it in any way. While she searched her mind for a way to explain this as delicately as possible, Laura had started speaking again.

'You do realise, don't you, Felicia, that the gallery is entirely my baby?' She paused for a moment, then cleared her throat. 'What I'm trying to say is that Adam has nothing to do with it, and that your . . .' she hesitated for a moment, then went on '. . . your personal situation with him won't come into it at all.'

'I see,' Felicia said non-committally. She wanted to tell Laura that there *was* no personal situation, but decided eventually that the less said the better.

'You surely know that he's not really that interested in art,' Laura went on. 'The gallery is only an investment to him, and as I told you before, he leaves it entirely in my hands. In fact, the last I heard he was in France on business.'

'All right, then,' said Felicia, relieved at that piece of news. 'It sounds wonderful. You go ahead and set a date some time during the week before Christmas, and I'll be ready.'

December, she thought, after they had hung up. It only gave her a little over a month to get ready. She'd have to work virtually non-stop, but that suited her perfectly. Not only would it take her mind off the fiasco with Adam, but it would also give her a good excuse to avoid any more embarrassing questions about it. Now, with a firm date for her show, she would have to hole in to get the work done in the short time that was left, and by then the whole thing would probably be forgotten.

For days, Adam's parting note to her burned a hole in her jacket pocket, where she had left it as a sort of punishment, a way to heap ashes on her head. From time to time she would retrieve the crumpled piece of paper and, with tears in her eyes and still hot with shame, re-read it once again.

Adam had won in the end anyway, and he had done it as he did everything else, with style and grace. Nowhere in the note was there a hint of accusation or self-pity or condemnation. If anything, it was filled with regret at what might have been, and she could hardly bear to think about that.

For the two weeks, Felicia lived like a virtual recluse, she and Felix and the plants, working practically non-stop to get ready for the show. Although Laura was an enormous help in deciding what to exhibit and persuading the owners of her works to loan them to the gallery for that one night, only Felicia herself could put the actual finishing touches on the things in progress.

During a good part of those busy weeks, she was in an agony of indecision whether to exhibit the bust she had done of Adam. The very worst part of that awful night she had straggled home from Miami was the sight of the finished model of his head still sitting there in her studio where she had left it. After the first sickening glance, she had draped a cloth over it and vowed never to look at it again.

As the days passed, however, she couldn't resist an occasional peep under the drapery. The trouble was, each time she did, she was more convinced than ever that it was by far her best work. She had captured him in a serious, rather brooding, thoughtful pose that revealed a facet of his personality not obvious to the casual observer; to her, it represented the essence of an ideal masculinity, regardless of the character of the man who had sat for it.

Then one day she found herself drawn to it once again, and before she realised what she was doing, she had mixed up a batch of plaster and started slathering it on. By the time she finished, several hours later, she knew she had to exhibit the bust at the show. Even if it was patently obvious who the model was, what difference did it make? She had the right to sculpt the head of anyone she chose, after all.

Finally, one day in early December, she suddenly felt sick and tired of her own company, and decided to call Carol to see if she was still even speaking to her after her long silence.

The moment she plugged in the telephone, it started to ring. When she answered it, an irate Carol immediately broke into a series of accusations.

'Well,' came the sarcastic voice, 'so you've finally decided to come out of hibernation and rejoin the human race! Really, Felicia, you've gone too far this time. I presume you've been hiding out, but the least you could do is call your oldest friend once in a while to let her know you're still alive!'

'I was just going to,' Felicia put in weakly when she finally got the chance. 'I'm really sorry, Carol, for shutting myself up this way, but I've been busy trying to get ready for the exhibition.'

'What exhibition?' Carol asked sullenly.

'Oh, didn't I tell you about it?' she said in an innocent tone. 'The gallery has asked me to get together a collection for a one-woman show later this month. I've been working like a dog. How have you been?' she rushed on, before Carol had the chance to start in on her again.

'Oh, all right.' There was a short silence, then, in a rather hushed tone, Carol asked, 'Have you heard from Adam?'

'No, of course not.'

'Do you want to talk about it?'

Felicia laughed shortly. 'There's nothing to talk about, Carol. I already told you, it just didn't work out, that's all.'

'You sound as though you think it's hopeless,' Carol said sympathetically.

'Oh, yes,' Felicia replied in a firm voice. 'There's no question of that.' She longed to ask her friend if she'd seen Adam around town during her seclusion, but in the end she decided that such a question wouldn't serve any purpose. Better to drop the whole subject. 'How about lunch later in the week?' she asked instead.

'Great! I'd love to.'

'Is Friday good for you?'

'Friday is fine. I'll stop by and get you.'

For the next two and a half weeks, Felicia threw herself into her work with a renewed sense of urgency. Not only was she working against a deadline that loomed ominously over her every waking moment, but her work had taken on the added dimension of escape from brooding over the shambles of her personal life.

She was sleeping badly too, and that didn't add anything to her state of nervous tension. No matter how hard she worked, nor how exhausted she was when she fell into bed, there was still what seemed like an endless period of time when she simply lay in bed, wide awake, staring up at the ceiling, totally unable to dismiss the tormenting thoughts that filled her mind.

Even if she had not deceived Adam, she knew quite well that there had never been even a remote possibility of a normal marriage, or children, with him. At best, all she could have hoped for was a brief affair. Wonderful while it lasted, perhaps, but devastating when it was over.

Even the thrill of the one-woman show was cold comfort during the long winter nights alone in her loft with only a cat and African violets for company. Work, she kept telling herself as she tossed and turned in her bed. Work was the only answer.

CHAPTER NINE

IT WAS snowing lightly the night of the show. On every street corner stood a red-suited Santa Claus, ringing his bell and shouting, 'Ho, ho, ho,' at the passers-by. Macys, Gimbels, Bloomingdales, all the large department stores were brightly lit, with colourful Christmas scenes in their windows.

The streets were jammed with traffic, last-minute shoppers in from Long Island and Connecticut, office workers staying in town after work to pick up one more gift. Christmas was only a week away, and it seemed that every resident of the five boroughs, as well as the neighbouring states, was in town.

Before leaving her apartment, Felicia went through yet another crisis of nerves. She and Laura had worked late last night putting the finishing touches to the exhibition. One of the smaller rooms at the back of the gallery had been set aside for her exclusive use, and when they were through, with each piece in place just where they had agreed beforehand, Felicia was positive it was all wrong.

She had begged Laura to start all over again but, after one long look, Laura had practically pushed her out of the door, telling her to go home and forget about it, it was perfect just the way it was, and besides, it was too late.

What if no one comes? Felicia agonised on the way over in the taxi that night. Last time hadn't been so bad. Tonight she would be on her own, the star turn, the focus of all attention, and she just didn't think she could bear it. For days she had pleaded with Laura to be let out of an appearance, using the same arguments she had tried in September about not being a performer.

But Laura had been adamant. 'You want to sell, don't you? Then you must show up. They want to meet you.'

'What if I get sick?'

'Then we'll postpone the show,' was the firm reply.

The invitations had specified an eight o'clock opening. It was now seven-thirty, and as Felicia got out of the taxi and walked towards the building, she had a moment's serious doubt that her legs would even carry her to the door, much less support her for three whole hours.

The gallery was brightly lit. Laura had decorated the front windows all in white and gold—tiny lights twinkling on a ceramic tree, gold velvet hangings, and a lovely Nativity scene with each figure finished in a matt glaze that glowed with life.

At the lovely sight, Felicia felt a certain sense of calm descend on her, covering her like a warm blanket. It was Christmas, after all, the season to count one's blessings and send up prayers of gratitude for her good fortune in having the show at all, instead of collapsing like an immature adolescent.

She rapped lightly on the glass door, and in a moment she heard the key in the lock and Laura appeared on the other side.

'Come in,' she invited. 'Glad you got here a little

early.'

'It's freezing out there,' Felicia commented, stepping inside.

When the door was locked behind her, Laura turned to her and gave her a swift, narrow-eyed glance. 'Are you OK?' she asked warily.

Felicia had to laugh at the worried frown on Laura's face. 'I'm fine,' she assured her. 'Now, at any rate.' She shrugged out of her heavy woollen coat and took off her gloves. 'Really, I'm fine. What can they do to me? I've done my best. Now it's up to them.'

Laura expelled a long sigh. 'Well, thank God for that!' she breathed. 'I was afraid I'd have to prop you up in a corner and feed you tranquillisers all night!'

'I'm sorry I've been such a trial to you, Laura,' Felicia said soberly. 'And I can't tell you how grateful I am to you for giving me this chance.'

Laura put a reassuring hand on her arm. 'Believe me, you weren't the worst of my problem children.' She shook her head. 'If I haven't learned by now how to handle temperamental artists, I'm in the wrong business. It goes with the territory. And I wouldn't have given you the chance if I didn't think you deserved it, so let's just forget it and go on to bigger and better things.'

'My own sentiments exactly,' said Felicia with a smile.

Laura took her coat, then stood back and gazed at her for a moment. 'You look wonderful,' she said. 'New dress?'

'Yes. Do you like it?' In an effort to distract herself from her nervousness, Felicia had gone shopping the day before. Unsure of her taste in clothes and hating shopping, especially in the Christmas rush, she had bought the first dress she'd tried on. The minute she put it on tonight, of course, it had seemed all wrong to her.

'I love it,' said Laura. 'That shade of red is perfect with your colouring, and the style just suits you—festive yet subdued, if you know what I mean.'

Felicia breathed a sigh of relief. 'Oh, good. I was so afraid it was too—oh, I don't know, *conspicuous,* I guess.'

She still felt a little uncomfortable in it. The wide scoop neck of the bodice still seemed a little too low-cut, the fit just a little too tight for comfort.

'Heavens, no,' said Laura with a laugh. 'You've got a good figure and marvellous colouring. Why not show them off?' She glanced at her watch. 'Want to take one last look at the exhibits before the guests arrive?'

'Yes, I guess I'd better.'

'No more changes, now,' Laura warned sternly as Felicia started walking towards the back of the gallery.

'Don't worry,' Felicia called back with a laugh, 'I think the crisis is over!'

The lights were on in the showroom, discreet wall sconces that showed each figurine off to perfect advantage. At one end of the narrow room was the Courtney boy's bronze head, her first attempt in that medium. Next was the long glass display case that held a collection of her ballerina figurines. Some were better than others, but she could see that she had steadily improved through the years.

It was then that she noticed the bust she had done

of Adam, set back in a corner with only a dim light burning off to one side. She herself had chosen that particular spot for its display, winning out in the end over Laura's heated objections.

Laura had argued in vain that the bronze bust was by far her best work, agreeing with Felicia's own private assessment, but in the end she had finally given in, apparently sensing at last that the reason for Felicia's insistence on the inconspicuous position in the show was more personal that it was artistic.

Felicia hadn't seen it for some weeks, and was hardly able to bear looking at it even now, it brought back so many painful memories. When the bronzer had finished, she had told him to deliver it right to the gallery, and as she gazed at it now, alone in the hushed room with only the faint sound of a Christmas carol drifting in from the street to be heard, she felt a sudden poignant pull at her heartstrings.

She wondered where Adam was, what he was doing, how he felt about her by now. Did he still hate her? She hadn't seen him or heard anything about him since Miami. Not only had she deliberately kept thoughts of him at bay, resisting them whenever they appeared, but there seemed to be a conspiracy of silence about him among her friends and family. Even Laura hadn't mentioned his name once during the weeks of planning for the show.

Perhaps he was still in France, she thought. Certainly, knowing him, he was embarked on yet another love affair, and a sudden sharp stab of jealousy of the unknown woman he was undoubtedly romantically involved with pierced her heart.

It could have been me, a little voice whispered. She wished with all her heart she'd had the courage to follow her feelings instead of giving in so blindly to her old fear of being hurt again, but it was too late now.

Just then she was startled out of her dismal reverie by the sound of voices coming from the main room of the gallery. Her heart started to pound erratically. The guests had arrived. Slowly, with one last, lingering look at the bronze head, she turned to greet them.

By half-past eleven it was almost over, and Felicia stood near the entrance to the gallery, saying good-night to the departing guests.

The evening had turned out to be a success beyond her wildest dreams. It seemed that everyone she knew had shown up—her whole family, Carol, old friends she hadn't seen for years, the entire ballet company, several of her former customers—as well as a great many people she didn't know. Future customers, she hoped.

Even her brother Jack and his wife came down from Boston, a remarkable tribute considering his busy practice, and Felicia took special pains to make them welcome and show her gratitude by spending as much time with them as she could spare.

'Well, little sister,' he said now, 'it's time we were on our way. It looks as though you've made quite a hit, and I must say I'm very proud of you.'

Coming from her busy, preoccupied brother, this was high praise indeed, and Felicia glowed with pleasure. 'I'm just glad you could come, Jack. You too, Martha,' she added, turning to her sister-in-law. 'I really appreciate . . .'

Just then the door opened, bringing a blast of cold air into the overheated gallery. Shivering a little, Felicia looked up in annoyance to see who would be coming this late, just when the show was about over. Then she froze in her tracks as the last person in the world she ever wanted to see again walked inside.

Adam! She looked around wildly for a place to hide. He was supposed to be in France. With him was a striking blonde woman. Although Felicia would have liked nothing better than to sink through the floor, she managed to plaster a rigid smile on her face.

Through the constant low hum of conversation buzzing about her, she dimly heard Adam's voice and her brother's as they greeted each other. Then she made out that Martha was asking her a question. She was so tense by now that every muscle in her body felt as though it had hardened into granite, and when she turned to Martha she was half afraid her stiff neck would crack in the process.

'I'm sorry,' she said in a falsely bright tone, 'I didn't hear you.'

'It's so noisy in here,' Martha said. 'I was wondering if you knew Elizabeth Proctor. She's an old schoolmate of mine from Boston.'

Felicia murmured a polite 'How do you do' and limply shook the blonde's outstretched hand. A fresh contingent of guests approached the door, and she was finally able to force her frozen limbs to move so she could thank them for coming and say goodnight. When they were gone, she stepped away from the

door and went to stand behind Jack.
Then she heard Adam's voice at her side. 'How have you been, Felicia?' he asked quietly.
She hadn't even looked at him after that first awful shock of recognition, and was now startled to find his face not inches away from hers, so close that she could see the faint bristles along his upper lip and hard jawline, and smell the familiar fragrance of the aftershave he used. His face seemed somewhat drawn to her, the mouth set, the creases at the corners of his eyes a little deeper.
'Fine,' she said. 'How about you?'
'Not bad,' he replied with a nod. There was a short silence. 'Your exhibition tonight seems to have been quite a success, judging by the crowd. Congratulations.'
'Thank you,' she said stiffly.
His glance swept over her in a swift appraisal. 'You're looking well. I like your dress—it suits you.'
Just then Elizabeth Proctor, his lovely blonde friend, came up to them. 'Shall we go now, Adam?' she asked, putting an arm through his. 'Or do you want to stay a little longer?'
'We can leave, if you'd like.' He turned back to Felicia. 'I really just wanted to put in an appearance at your show. It looks to be financially successful, at any rate.'
'Yes,' she replied with a tight smile. 'And that's the important thing, isn't it?'
Adam raised his eyebrows slightly, then gave her a curt bow, and walked off with his blonde.
As Felicia watched the tall figure make its way through the crowd and out the front entrance, the

first faint stirrings of the old resentment began to rise up in her. After all, she thought, *he* had actually left *her* in Miami. Granted that her own plans had been pretty underhanded, still the fact remained that she hadn't gone through with them.

All that guilt, she thought disgustedly. All that regret—wasted! Here he was, only a month after the débâcle in Miami, a beautiful blonde on his arm, acting as though he owned the world.

Then she heard her brother calling to her impatiently. 'We've got to go, Felicia.'

She walked over to the door. 'Thanks again for coming, you two. I really do appreciate it.'

Martha turned to her. 'Felicia,' she said in a low voice, 'I don't know what the situation is between you and Adam, but I want you to know that I'm certain there's nothing between him and Elizabeth Proctor. They're just old family friends.'

Felicia laughed. 'It doesn't matter in the slightest, Martha, but thanks, anyway.'

'Damn playboy!' she heard Jack mutter under his breath.

Martha turned on him. 'Now, Jack, that isn't fair,' she said sharply. 'Adam may have had his share of flings, but why shouldn't he? To my knowledge, he's never treated a woman badly or promised more than he was willing to deliver. I was only trying to reassure Felicia that if there was any hope for their marriage, Adam wasn't going to be the one to spoil it by getting involved with Elizabeth behind her back.'

It was an amazing speech for her to make, and both Jack and Felicia stared at her, open-mouthed. Finally Jack waved a hand in the air and glared at his wife.

'Well, I'm sorry,' he said huffily. 'I stand corrected. I don't really care two cents about Adam St John's private life, to tell you the truth. All I'm concerned about is my sister.'

Felicia could only stand there, stunned at Jack's ringing defence of her rights. 'Listen, you two,' she said firmly. 'There's no point in your getting into a marital squabble over me. Let's just forget it. Believe me, the marriage never had a chance, and it's as much my fault as it is Adam's. In fact,' she added, 'probably more.'

She thanked them again, said goodnight, and watched as Jack hurried Martha out of the door before the discussion could start again.

Half an hour later, everyone had finally gone, and Laura had just locked the door behind the last straggler. Felicia collapsed on the one comfortable chair in the main gallery and looked up at her as she eased herself down on a chair opposite.

'Oh, my aching feet!' she groaned, taking off her shoes. She gave Felicia a broad grin. 'Well, congratulations are in order. You made a pretty penny tonight from the pieces that were for sale, and,' she added, riffling her notebook, 'I have enough orders here to keep you busy for months to come.'

Felicia sighed happily. 'It *was* a success, wasn't it?'

'Very definitely,' Laura replied.

The two women sat in silence for some moments, both of them basking in the afterglow of the wonderful evening. Finally, Felicia stretched widely and rose from her chair.

'If I don't get packed up and get out of here, I'm

going to have to spend the night,' she said, stifling a yawn.

'Oh, don't bother with that tonight. The gallery is quite safe.' Laura slipped her shoe back on and stood up. 'Why not leave the packing up for a few days? Who knows, we may get another paying customer or two in here tomorrow.'

'All right, I guess I will. There are just one or two small pieces I set aside for my family's Christmas gifts that I'd like to take home with me tonight.'

'Sure, go ahead. I'll just go straighten up at the bar. I can't believe the champagne those art-lovers manage to consume! How about a last glass?'

'No, thanks. That would *really* put me to sleep!'

While Laura switched off the bright overhead lights in the main area of the gallery, Felicia made her way back into the small room where her own exhibition had been held, and once again viewed each separate piece with a thrill of pleasure.

They're like the children I'll never have, she mused, and with that thought, a sudden sadness began to rise up in her. Her joy at the evening's triumph slowly started to dissipate, and an insidious depression threatened to engulf her.

Slowly she walked over to the glass display case against the long wall and stared down at the pieces displayed inside. Could they really take the place of her own children? Was it really too late to live a normal life? Did a career necessarily mean that she had to renounce love, marriage, a home? She felt so dreadfully *alone* all of a sudden.

She had chosen a graceful ballerina figurine for her mother's Christmas gift. It was modelled loosely on

Irina Petrovska, a slight figure in a short tutu, standing on her toes, her arms poised gracefully over her head. The head was bent, the eyes closed, and her mother had admired it extravagantly tonight, not knowing that Felicia had already decided to give it to her. All she had to do now was take it home and wrap it. It would make her feel better to *do* something, she thought, anything at all just to shake her black mood.

But just as she was reaching inside the case to lift out the delicate ballerina, she found her gaze travelling down the length of the room to the corner where she had placed Adam's bronze head.

Two or three people had been interested in buying it tonight, but she had put each one of them off. For some reason, she couldn't bear to part with it. In a sense, it belonged to Adam anyway. He had offered to buy it from her, and she had refused. She hadn't had another made for him. If things had been different, perhaps she would have made him a present of it.

She walked over and stared fixedly down at it, as though trying to fathom its secrets or to find an answer to her dilemma in the uplifted face. Once again she wondered what she had seen in the man himself that she could have created the statue with such love.

As she viewed it with some detachment now, the thought struck her that if she were seeing it for the first time as someone else's work, her immediate reaction would be that the artist had been in love with the model. Only love could have found just that expression on his face, just those characteristics to emphasise.

She reached out a hand and ran it over the smooth, cold metal, the wide cheekbones, the firm, strong nose, the fine mouth and bony jaw. But she hadn't been in love with Adam, had she? She'd adored the ideal he embodied, not the man himself. But what was the difference? Didn't it amount to the same thing? If she had seen qualities in Adam that struck the spark needed to set her creative impulse on fire, then perhaps she had loved the man himself as well.

Had he loved Adam? Her mind went back to the weeks he had sat for her—his patience, his good nature. And his persistent wooing of her. That was what it had been, she realised for the first time. What she had seen as a deliberate, calculated seduction had actually been a sort of courtship. Why then had she rejected it? And in so brutal and childish a fashion?

Seeing Adam tonight, just for that brief moment, had brought it all back again, all the regrets, all the memories she thought she had buried so successfully in the past month. She wondered if Martha was right about Elizabeth Proctor. Were they just old friends?

Felicia sighed deeply, then turned to go. As she switched out the light, and the room was suddenly plunged in darkness, she shivered in the warm room. She'd give anything, she thought, to turn back the clock and do it all over again.

CHAPTER TEN

THE NEXT morning, Felicia was awakened out of a sound sleep by a shrill ringing sound directly in her right ear. With a groan, she opened her eyes and fumbled for the telephone on the table beside her bed.

'Hello,' she muttered.

It was Laura. 'Did I wake you up?'

Felicia rolled over and blinked at the shaft of sunlight that was pouring in through the widow. She had been too worked up about the show to sleep when she had gone to bed the night before, and had tossed and turned half the night. In between bouts of elation over her success, Adam's face kept appearing before her, each time bringing with it the same dead weight in the pit of her stomach. She had finally fallen into an exhausted sleep around four o'clock in the morning.

'What time is it?' she asked groggily.

'It's after ten. I just called to give you the latest results.' Laura went on with a brief rundown on the specific sales from the show. 'And orders are still coming in this morning,' she said happily. Then she added casually, 'Oh, yes, and the bronze head has sold as well.'

Felicia sat up in bed. 'The bronze head? You mean the Courtney boy? There must be some mistake. The Courtneys already own it.'

'Not the Courtney boy, the other one—you know, the man.' She hesitated a second, then coughed delicately. 'Adam.'

'Laura, you can't do that! I told you I hadn't made up my mind yet whether I even wanted to sell it.'

'It fetched a pretty penny, Felicia,' said Laura, naming a high figure. 'Already paid for. I have a cheque for your share right here in front of me.'

'I don't care! You'll just have to call them and tell them you made a mistake. And whatever you do, don't let that statue get out of the gallery.'

'I'm afraid it's too late for that,' Laura told her. 'It's already gone.'

Felicia got out of bed and started pacing around the room, so angry by now she could hardly speak. She couldn't bear the thought of some stranger owning that head.

'Laura, you had no *right* to sell it without my permission. I want you to get it back.'

'I'm sorry. Felicia, I can't do that.'

'Why not?' In her panic, Felicia's voice had risen gradually, until she was almost shouting by now. 'Who has it? If you won't get it back for me, I'll do it myself.'

'Now, calm down,' Laura said soothingly. 'What's the big deal? You still have the plaster mould, you can take another casting. I explained to the buyer that there would probably be other copies made.'

'Laura, I don't *want* to make any more castings. And even if I did, that's not the point. It's *that* casting I don't want to sell. Now, tell me who bought it, and I'll speak to them myself.'

'I can't do that.'

'Why not?'

'I promised to keep the buyer's name confidential. He was quite insistent on that point.'

'Do you mean to tell me I'm not to know who bought my own work?' It didn't make any sense. Who would Laura protect to the point where she wouldn't tell her . . .

Then of course she knew. She sank slowly back down on to the edge of the bed. It had to be. Adam himself was the only person who would make such a stipulation. He had wanted to buy the bust while she was still working on it.

'It was Adam, wasn't it?' she said at last in a dull, lifeless tone.

'I didn't tell you that,' Laura said hastily.

'No, Laura, you didn't.'

They hung up then, and Felicia went into the kitchen to make a pot of coffee. It had stopped snowing, and a pale sun glistened on the ice crystals that had formed overnight along the sides of the ploughed street below.

She stood at the window in her robe, sipping slowly at her coffee and debating what she should do. She supposed Adam had a right to the bust; at one time she had even considered making him a present of it. But she certainly couldn't take any money for it, and the sum Laura had named was the exact figure she had quoted him when they had first discussed the bust of Irina.

Finally she made up her mind. She walked briskly into the bathroom to shower and get herself ready for the ordeal that lay ahead.

Two hours later she was riding up in the lift to the

twentieth floor of an elegant old co-op apartment building on Central Park West, overlooking the snow-covered park itself, and practising her speech as she was borne upwards. She hadn't called first, afraid Adam would tell her not to come. It was Sunday, a little before noon, and chances were he would be at home.

She had dressed carefully, in a new black suit that looked very sedate and businesslike, a plain white blouse that tied at the neck and fur-lined boots. On the way, she had stopped briefly at the gallery to pick up the cheque from a chastened Laura, and even managed to browbeat Adam's address out of her.

All that morning she had been debating simply mailing him the cheque instead of going to him, but in the end had decided it would be better to do it in person. Not only did she want to make sure he took the money, she desperately hoped for a chance to try to make some kind of peace with him. She certainly had no illusions that he would ever desire her again, but she didn't want him to be her enemy. After all, they were still legally married, and something would have to be done about a divorce or an annulment sooner or later.

When the lift slid to a stop and the doors opened, she stepped out into a wide foyer paved in black and white tiles. There was a graceful Queen Anne table on the long wall in front of her, a vase of red roses sitting on top of it. And there, standing beside it and leaning up against an open doorway, was Adam, his hands in the pockets of his dark trousers. He was wearing a white dress shirt, the top button undone, the sleeves rolled up to his elbows.

The doorman had called Falicia's name up before allowing her to get past him, so she knew he was expecting her. Still, she was surprised to see him waiting for her, and her heart lurched painfully at the sight of him. He looked wonderful, tanned and fit, but as he walked towards her, she was struck once again by the drawn look about the eyes she had noticed last night at the gallery.

'Hello, Felicia,' he said. 'What brings you here?'

He took his hands out of his pockets and crossed his arms over his chest, his cold blue-grey eyes never leaving her face, and suddenly she knew she'd been a fool to come here this way. She fought down the impulse to turn around and make a dash for the lift and a quick exit. But there was no escape now. She would just have to get her business over with as soon as possible get out of there.

'Hello, Adam,' she said. She reached in her handbag and took out the envelope with the cheque in it, then walked slowly towards him. 'I came to return your cheque, the money you paid for the statue.' She took it out of the envelope and held it out to him.

Adam didn't move. He merely flicked a glance at the cheque, as though it were an offensive bit of trash, then said evenly, 'I don't want it.'

Her hand dropped to her side. 'Well, neither do I. I told you a long time ago I didn't want you to pay for the bust.'

He obviously wasn't even going to meet her half-way, and it was quite clear that there was no hope he'd ever forgive her. She didn't know what to say, what to do, so she did the first thing that came to her mind and tore the cheque across twice and laid the pieces on the table.

'I can always write another,' Adam said promptly. He tilted his head slightly and gazed at her for a long moment. His eyes travelled over her in a sweeping appraisal, then came back up to search her face carefully. 'Why don't you come inside and we'll talk about it,' he said quietly.

Totally taken aback at the sudden change in tone, Felicia could only stare for a moment. 'All right,' she said at last, and walked past him through the open doorway.

As he closed the door and followed her inside, she looked around at the enormous sitting-room, and it struck her immediately that it was a perfect reflection of the man himself. The greyish carpet and dark blue upholstered furniture were elegant and subdued, yet there were bright flashes of colour in the paintings on the white walls, and the bank of windows at the far end looked out upon a sweeping view of the park and the city.

When he came to stand beside her, she turned to him. 'What a lovely room, Adam,' she said. 'I'm impressed.'

'I'm happy to hear that.' There was a touch of irony in his tone. 'If you recall, I did my best to get you here once before.'

Felicia flushed at the painful reminder and took a step away from him. 'I was surprised to see you at the gallery last night,' she said, just to change the subject. 'I thought you were still in France, or wherever.'

Adam's eyes widened. 'I came back from France

weeks ago. And as for last night, it *is* my gallery, after all.'

'But Laura said . . .'

'I don't feel obliged to inform Laura of all my plans,' he broke in smoothly. 'Besides,' he went on, taking a step towards her and closing the gap between them, 'I had a perfect right to be at your show. I'm still your husband, after all.'

Felicia's muscles tensed at the sneering tone in his voice, and she looked away. 'Oh, please,' she said bitterly, 'don't bring up that farce.'

He gave her a look of mock surprise. 'Farce? How can you call it a farce, Felicia? It was a legal marriage, still binding.' His mouth curled in a parody of a smile. 'Till death us do part, remember?'

'I'm trying hard to forget.' It was time to make her peace-offering. She had to get it over with before she lost control and they started shouting at each other. She looked down at her feet, frowning, trying to remember the speeches she had practised. Finally she decided she would just have to plunge ahead and hope for the best.

'Adam,' she began hesitantly. Her voice cracked, and she cleared her throat nervously and tried again. 'Adam, after what's happened, I know we can never be friends, but . . .'

'You're damned right,' he snapped. 'We can't!'

Her heart sank at the harsh tone in his voice, the finality of his words. The blue-grey eyes were hooded, his face devoid of expression, and he stood absolutely motionless before her. What more was there for her to say? He was implacable.

'All right,' she said at last. She spread her hands

wide and shrugged defeatedly. 'I had to give it a try. Now I guess the best thing is for me to leave.'

She started to walk past him towards the door, but he was still standing directly in front of it, barring her way.

'That's it, then?' he said. 'That's all you have to say to me?'

'What more *can* I say? I'm sorry. I'd hoped we could at least be civil to each other. I felt I should at least try once more to explain to you what happened, but you're obviously in no mood to listen.' As she met his cool, challenging gaze, a slow indignation began to rise up in her. She lifted her chin. 'Although I don't know what made me think you might. You refused to hear me out that night in Miami, after all. Oh, no, you turned around and ran at the mere *thought* that one woman in the world might not be eternally grateful to be allowed to fall into your bed.' She pointed an accusing finger at him. 'Don't ever forget that. You left me!'

Both black eyebrows shot up at that. 'I don't know what you've got to be so resentful about,' said Adam angrily. 'After all, *you* were the one who hatched that rotten little trick on *me*.' He shook his head sadly. 'And to think I trusted you to honour the bargain we'd made! Things have come to a pretty pass when a man can't trust his own wife!'

By now she was well aware that the corners of his mouth had begun to twitch. 'Adam!' she cried, glaring at him. 'Will you please stop that?' Every word he uttered cut through her like a knife, and he seemed to be *enjoying* the whole thing. 'You've already had your revenge. Now please, just let me leave.'

To her utter horror, she heard her voice crack, felt her throat tighten and the tears sting her eyes. In the next moment they began to spill over, and she turned from him and buried her face in her hands.

As she choked back the sobs that threatened, there was utter silence in the room. Not even the noises of the city on the street below filtered through the heavy double-glazed windows, and when she gave a loud sniff it seemed to echo in the high-ceilinged room.

Then she heard his footsteps approaching, and felt his presence behind her. She waited, hardly daring to breathe, wondering if this time he really would strike her. But nothing happened, and after a few moments she wiped her eyes on the back of her hand, fumbled for a tissue in her bag and blew her nose loudly.

She had just started to turn around, resolved to rush past him and *walk* down the entire twenty floors if she had to, when she felt a restraining hand on her arm. She shuddered a little at his touch, then flinched and started to pull away from him, but his grip only tightened. Felicia stood stock still, holding herself rigid with apprehension at what awful thing he might say or do, and feeling that whatever it was, she probably deserved it.

'Why did you do it, Felicia?' he said softly. She couldn't face him, couldn't utter a word. 'Why did you break our agreement?' he went on. 'Didn't the fact that I married you—*married* you, for God's sake—mean anything to you? Do you have any idea how hard I've fought to steer clear of that?'

She turned slowly to face him. 'And do you have any idea what it feels like to be just a—a—just a warm *body* to be bargained over? Come on, Adam, admit it. You're trying to make our marriage out to be a serious commitment on your part, a great concession to me personally, when we both know darned well it meant absolutely nothing to you except a way to get me into bed. You're just being a poor sport now because it didn't work.'

'Well, Felicia, tell me something. What did it mean to you? I realise I was pretty dense about the whole thing, but even I had a vague suspicion all along that you might be planning some kind of tricky move. You accuse me of marrying you just to get you into bed, but what about you? Wasn't the only reason you agreed to our bargain—which, by the way, you never had any intention of honouring—so that you could finish that damned bust?'

They stood there, not a foot apart, glaring at each other for several seconds. Felicia couldn't think of one sensible thing to say. It was all such a dreadful, hopeless mess.

Suddenly a great wave of weariness passed over her, and her whole body went slack. 'What's the point of arguing about it, Adam?' she asked quietly. 'It's over and done with. I'm sorry if I behaved badly, but I don't think I'm solely at fault here. If you hadn't pursued me so relentlessly in such an insulting manner . . .'

'Insulting!' Adam broke in. He shook his head slowly from side to side. 'Do you honestly believe that *any* woman would be worth marrying just to go to bed with her? Believe me, that little scheme has been tried on me long before you came along, and I was well inoculated against such foolishness years before I met you.'

'All right!' she cried. 'You're so determined to make yourself out to be the innocent party here, tell me something. Just why did you marry me, then?'

He gave her a quizzical look. 'Can't you figure it out for yourself?'

'I wouldn't be asking if I could do that, now, would I?' she demanded angrily. 'As far as I'm concerned, you're just like all the rest, and nothing you've ever said or done has made me think otherwise.' She nodded vigorously. 'Yes. You're exactly like . . .'

'Like who, Felicia?' he said sharply. 'Just like who? The guy who burned you so badly in the first place?'

Felicia gave him a startled look. 'No, of course not. That has nothing to do with it.'

'Then there *was* someone—I thought as much! And you've judged all men ever since by that one bad experience.'

'Now listen, Adam,' she said heatedly, 'you're twisting everything around. All right, I was hurt once, a long time ago, but as far as I'm concerned, in the whole time I've known you, you've never said or done one single thing to make me think you were any different. From the first moment we met, you had one thing on your mind, and you never made any bones about it.'

'And you don't find that flattering?'

'I most certainly do not!' she retorted. 'That's not my style, and definitely not my idea of the basis for marriage. All I ever was to you was a challenge. You only wanted me because you couldn't have me.'

'All right,' he said, frowning, 'I admit that was my intention at the beginning.'

'Aha!' she cried, vindicated at last. She jerked her arm out of his grasp, turned away from him and stared blindly out of the window.

'Look at me, Felicia,' said Adam sternly. When she continued to gaze stonily ahead, he put his hands on her shoulders and pulled her roughly around to face him. 'I said look at me, damn it,' he ground out between clenched teeth.

'You're hurting me!' she protested.

With a sigh of exasperation, he dropped his hands to his sides. 'God knows why I'm even bothering trying to explain anything to you,' he muttered under his breath. 'What you need is a good beating.' Then, with a deep sigh, he said, 'Just tell me one thing, Felicia. Why did you come here today?'

His eyes bored into her. She bit her lip and looked down at her feet. It would cost her all her pride, and would shatter all her defences, but she had to say it now or it would be too late. She took a deep breath, summoned up all her courage, and plunged ahead.

'Adam, what I've been trying to tell you—what I tried to tell you that night in Miami—is that I wasn't going to go through with it.'

He eyed her suspiciously. 'What do you mean?'

'I mean that I'd changed my mind. If you hadn't stalked out of there like some kind of wounded lion, I wouldn't have used that ticket you found in my bag. I would have stayed with you. I would have . . .'

'Ah!' he said, expelling a long breath. 'That's what I wanted to hear you say.'

Felicia gave him a bleak look. Of course! Now his revenge was complete.

The dazzling eyes were burning into her, devouring her. Then they softened imperceptibly and Adam smiled for the first time that day. He held out his hand and said, 'Come and sit down. Now I've got something to say.'

He led her over to a long low couch set at a right angle to the fireplace and facing the window. As she moved, the sun glinting on the snow-covered trees in the park across the way flashed into her eyes, blinding her for a moment, and she squinted against it.

When she could see again, they had reached the couch and Adam was pulling her down beside him. Then, still holding her hand in both of his, he turned to her and began to speak in a low, earnest tone.

'I guess I can't really blame you for doubting my motives. I came on pretty strong, and the more you resisted, the more I wanted you. I never saw that as an insult, though. I never meant to degrade you in any way. It wasn't my intention to play house with you for a while and then leave you.'

'Well then, Adam,' she said helplessly, 'what *was* your intention? I don't understand you at all.'

'You felt I only wanted to use you, but I tried to tell you, to show you, in every way I could, that you meant much more to me than that. Wasn't it obvious to you how much I cared? I didn't think I could make it any clearer.'

At his words, a brief mental picture flashed into Felicia's mind, a sudden memory of the time they had spent together, his unfailing courtesy, his consideration, the fact that wherever they were, no matter what the temptations offered him by other women, he'd always had eyes only for her. She remembered too the night she had fainted dead away in the hotel room in Miami, and the look of genuine concern on his face when she had come to.

But most important of all, overriding everything else, were her own feelings for him, feelings she had never really dared face until just this moment. She'd admitted to herself a long time ago that she desired him. Now she had no choice but to acknowledge her love for this man, the love that was so transparently revealed in the bronze head she had made.

She looked at him. Was it possible? Did he really care? Was it safe to love him, to trust him? Most of all, was it too late?

'Adam,' she managed to choke out at last, 'what are you trying to say?'

He raised a hand and rubbed it over the back of his neck, then stared past her into the empty fireplace, frowning. When he turned to look at her again his eyes were glazed with intense emotion.

'I'm very much afraid, Felicia,' he said slowly, 'that at some point along our stormy path, I fell in love with you.'

A great surge of hope filled her heart. 'Then why in the world didn't you tell me?' she asked softly. 'Didn't you realise it would have made all the difference to me?'

'As I tried to explain to you a few minutes ago,' he said helplessly, 'I thought I had.'

'Oh, Adam, maybe it was my fault, my own fear of being burned again, but I needed to hear the words. I think every woman does.'

'Yes,' he said, 'I can see that now, and probably I was wrong not to make myself clearer. But try to understand. You were raised in a large, warm, loving family. I had elderly parents who must have loved me in their way, but were incapable of showing the slightest affection for any child, much less the noisy, rowdy boy I turned out to be.' He shrugged. 'If you've never received love, how can you be expected to recognise it when it comes along?'

He reached out for her then and took her into his arms, pulling her towards him. As his mouth came down on hers, the fireworks started going off inside her head and the very blood in her veins seemed to burst into flame. She leaned against him with a sigh, and felt his soft breath in her ear.

'I do love you, darling,' he murmured. 'Won't you give me another chance?'

Everything in her yearned to give herself to him, to ask no questions, to simply submit to the impulses that were building within her. She knew now that she would give him anything he asked of her, but first there was something she had to find out.

She pulled back a little from his seeking mouth. 'Just tell me one thing,' she said. Adam quirked an enquiring eyebrow. 'What would you have done if you *hadn't* found that plane ticket in my bag that night in Miami?'

'Why, come back and taken you to bed, of course,' he said without hesitation. 'After all, we *were* married.' Then he added in a low, husky voice, 'And we still are. For ever.'

His mouth came down on hers then, warm and seeking, as his hands stroked up and down her body. Adam loves me! The words sang in her head, and she pressed herself against him eagerly, opening her mouth to him, drinking in the taste of him, revelling in his touch.

Then she felt his hand under her jacket, fumbling with the buttons of her blouse. 'I do love you, darling, and I want to stay married to you,' he murmured against her mouth, as his other hand came up and tightened over her breast. 'Shall we try again for a wedding night?'

Felicia sat there, motionless, hardly breathing, as the last button was undone and he pulled blouse and jacket over her shoulders. He gazed down at her half-naked form, his eyes gleaming with desire.

'God, I want you, Felicia,' he said in a harsh voice. 'Say you want me too.'

'Oh, Adam, I do want you,' she breathed. 'And I do love you.'

His arms came around her then, and he held her as though he'd never let her go. 'Come on, then, wife,' he said, 'let's go to bed.'

He picked her up and carried her out of the room and down a long hallway, then into another room. She had the vague impression of a very large, very neat, very masculine bedroom, but her head was swimming so she didn't take in any details. He kissed her again, and laid her down on a wide bed. Then, slowly and deliberately, he removed the last of her clothing.

'You're so beautiful,' he breathed, running his hands over her bare skin. 'Exactly as I imagined you would be.'

She watched him as he took off his own clothes, throwing them carelessly at the foot of the bed, until finally he stood before her, strong and beautiful in his masculine nakedness, just as *she* had imagined *he* would be, and even as he sank down towards her, she knew that some day she would have to sculpt him that way.

With his hands and his mouth he worshipped her body, until finally they were joined together and became one at last, truly husband and wife.

Later, as she lay curled against Adam's long, powerful body, still glowing from his passionate love-making, Felicia thought of the time she had wasted with her fears and suspicions of him, time when they could have been together like this.

She raised herself up carefully so as not to disturb him, and looked down at her sleeping husband by the faint afternoon light filtering through the heavy curtains at the window. The sheet had tangled around his waist, leaving his upper body bare, and both the sculptor and the woman in her savoured the sight of the broad shoulders, the powerful muscles of his arms and chest.

Sinking back down on the pillow, she put a hand lightly around his waist and laid her cheek on his back. He had taught her how to love again just when she was sure that part of her life was over, and she would be forever grateful to him for that.

My husband, she thought happily, nestling against him. My model for love.

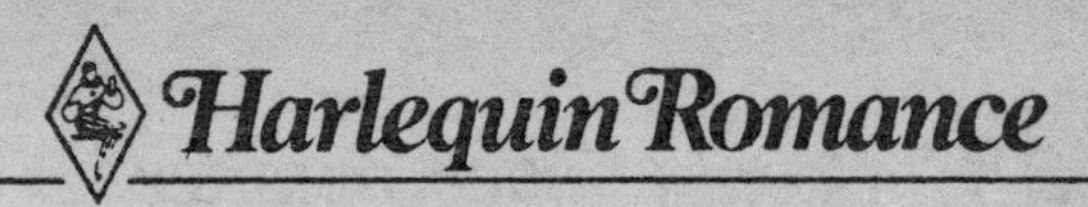

Coming Next Month

2971 REMEMBER, IN JAMAICA Katherine Arthur
For three years Claire has battled with her boss over his violent temper, impossible dreams and insane schedules. Suddenly, once she agrees to the working trip in Jamaica, Terrill changes into a pussycat. Claire can't help feeling suspicious.

2972 NO LOVE IN RETURN Elizabeth Barnes
The only reason Eve has worked as a model is to pay for her brother's education. To the imperious Jackson Sinclair, however, *model* is synonymous with *gold digger*. And there seems to be no way to persuade him he's wrong.

2973 SNOWFIRE Dana James
Beth can't pass up the chance to be official photographer on an Iceland expedition, though she's stunned to find her estranged husband, Dr. Allan Bryce, as leader. Even more shocking is the realization that Allan thinks he was the injured party!

2974 SYMPATHETIC STRANGERS Annabel Murray
Recently widowed Sandra begins to build a new life for herself and her young twins by helping friends of her mother's in Kent. Yet when lord of the manor Griff Faversham pursues her, she refuses to consider marriage to another wealthy man.

2975 BED, BREAKFAST & BEDLAM Marcella Thompson
In helping Bea McNair establish an Ozark Mountain retreat for Bea's ailing friends, Janet dismisses Lucas McNair's plan to move his mother to a Little Rock retirement home. There's no dismissing Lucas, though, when he descends upon her like a wrathful God.

2976 MOWANA MAGIC Margaret Way
Ally can't deny the attraction between herself and the powerful Kiall Lancaster, despite his mistrust of her. Common sense tells her to leave. But first she determines to straighten out Kiall's chauvinistic attitude. Not an easy task!

Available in April wherever paperback books are sold, or through Harlequin Reader Service:

In the U.S.
901 Fuhrmann Blvd.
P.O. Box 1397
Buffalo, N.Y. 14240-1397

In Canada
P.O. Box 603
Fort Erie, Ontario
L2A 5X3

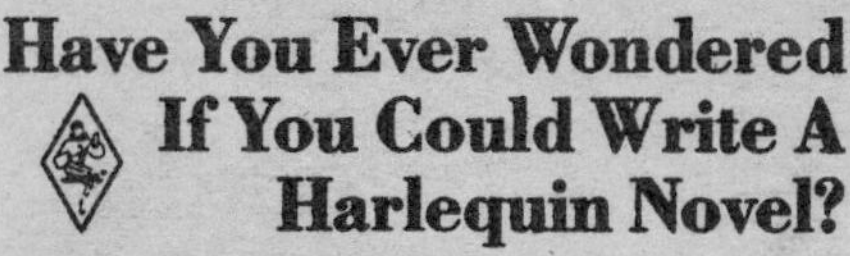

Have You Ever Wondered If You Could Write A Harlequin Novel?

Here's great news—Harlequin is offering a series of cassette tapes to help you do just that. Written by Harlequin editors, these tapes give practical advice on how to make your characters—and your story—come alive. There's a tape for each contemporary romance series Harlequin publishes.

Mail order only

All sales final

TO: *Harlequin Reader Service*
Audiocassette Tape Offer
P.O. Box 1396
Buffalo, NY 14269-1396

I enclose a check/money order payable to HARLEQUIN READER SERVICE® for $9.70 ($8.95 plus 75¢ postage and handling) for EACH tape ordered for the total sum of $______________ *
Please send:

- ☐ Romance and Presents
- ☐ American Romance
- ☐ Superromance
- ☐ Intrigue
- ☐ Temptation
- ☐ All five tapes ($38.80 total)

Signature______________________________
(please print clearly)
Name:______________________________
Address:______________________________
State:________________ Zip:______________

*Iowa and New York residents add appropriate sales tax.

AUDIO-H